"Any fifty-million-dollar bills in there?"

Rule's tone was uncharacteristically irritable. That scent of Mandy's was tormenting him, and he had a foolish urge to nuzzle the calf that kept grazing his hair as she steadied herself on his shoulders.

Mandy leaned forward to look into the tree hole. "Nothing," she said, then added, "Do you think you could get me down from here with a *little* more finesse than last time?"

"I can only try." Reaching up to grasp her waist, he lowered her slowly. Every centimeter of her hips, stomach and breasts was forced to brush against him. It seemed like an eternity before her feet touched the earth.

"Was that better?" he asked somewhat grimly.

Feeling feverish and light-headed, Mandy shot him a suspicious look. She was almost certain he'd deliberately made her aware of his undeniable attributes, but there *was* the remote possibility that he'd merely lowered her *very* carefully. Prudently swallowing her accusations, she remarked, "I'm impressed. If all else fails, you can always get a job as a forklift."

Renee Roszel Wilson's career as a romance writer began when her two sons started school. She'd gone out in search of a job in advertising and public relations because that's what she'd done before getting married. Unfortunately, she discovered some people believe that "once a woman rinses out a diaper she's lost half her brain cells." Feeling like "a pro-football player with bad knees," she took what was left of her gray matter and tackled the romance market. And she's never looked back!

Now Renee happily divides her time between teaching aerobics in Wichita and writing imaginative romances such as *Another Heaven*, her first Temptation. It took her four or five months to complete the book. "Agonizing," she says, "takes time."

Another Heaven
RENEE ROSZEL

Harlequin Books

TORONTO • NEW YORK • LONDON
AMSTERDAM • PARIS • SYDNEY • HAMBURG
STOCKHOLM • ATHENS • TOKYO • MILAN

For Doug
with love

Published April 1989

ISBN 0-373-25346-X

1

EVEN THE ELEMENTS seemed to know a treasure hunt worth millions was about to begin. A dense fog had been swept away, and the day was bright, alive with tense anticipation. Wind swept over the island, sending branches of the weeping beeches clawing at the sky. Ocean spray, carried on the gusts, spilled across the wall of the bride's garden, pelting Mandy's cheeks with salty kisses.

Trying to shake off her feeling of foreboding, she brushed away the dampness with the back of her hand. The heirs would be arriving within the hour, and she was running late. She dropped the garden shears in the basket beside the silver roses she'd just picked and swiped at the dirt on the seat of her jeans.

Nestling the basket in the crook of her arm, she pushed through the garden's gate. Hinges rusty from the constant bombardment of salt spray complained loudly. She made a mental note to tell the gardener to oil them. With a melancholy twinge, she wondered if the new owner of Barren Heath Isle, whoever that might prove to be, would even care about her gardens.

She headed up the stone path toward the mansion's kitchen entrance. Built of brick and painted eggshell white, the three-story manor was an imposing structure with an air of ancient Greece about it. Yet for all its grandeur, Mandy preferred the coziness of the caretaker's cottage she shared with her father-in-law, Papa

Josh. It was such a shame that their secure little refuge would soon be lost to them.

"Why, it's Mrs. McRae!" a gravelly voice called from some distance away.

Startled at hearing her name, Mandy turned to see Gavin Perth, the late Lydia Danforth's lawyer, beckoning for her to join him. He stood beneath one of the ancient mulberry trees that towered over the estate's formal gardens. She was appalled to see that he was not alone.

"Oh, no . . ." she breathed, self-consciously brushing back a wisp of hair. She hadn't intended to be caught in her work clothes, her hair pulled back hurriedly into one braid. She'd hoped to be presentable when she met Lydia and Arnold's family. But with Mr. Perth's hailing and waving, she had little choice but to meet them now.

Besides Gavin, there were three men and a woman clustered in the shade. Apparently Lydia's yacht had made excellent time from Portland. Mandy frowned, perplexed, and counted again. Four heirs? She'd thought there were to be five. She wondered what had happened to the missing person.

Forcing a smile, she waved back. Even from that distance, she could hear Mr. Perth explain that Mandy was a landscape architect hired to renovate grounds that had gradually become derelict.

It only took her a moment to cross the lawn and reach one of the meandering paths through the formal gardens, though they could hardly be called formal now. More a haven for sweet whimsy. A sloping sweep of contrasts, the gardens flowed in artful disorder around a manmade stream of Mandy's design. As she crossed a dainty, vermilion bridge, the stream gurgled and swirled beneath her feet.

The island's lawn and gardens had been a shambles—much like her life—when Mandy had come here. She felt a familiar pang at the memories but wrestled them back.

When she reached the group, Mandy realized she'd been wrong. One of the people she'd thought was a man was actually a woman dressed for a safari. Her hair was tucked up beneath a pith helmet, except for a few dangling, silver strands. She wore a khaki shirt, slacks and stout hiking boots. Curious, Mandy mused. Pulling her eyes away, she addressed Mr. Perth. "Hi, counselor. May I be of some assistance?"

"Ah, Mrs. McRae. I merely wanted to allow our guests to bask in your loveliness, since they were being so complimentary of your delightful garden." Gavin Perth, with his judiciously trimmed salt-and-pepper beard, looked as if he'd had his spine starched as heavily as his white shirts, smiled. "You are as enchanting a vision as those exquisite roses you're carrying."

She cast him a skeptical look. "Why, thank you, Mr. Perth. I've always admired a man with a sense of humor." She knew she looked about as enchanting as an unwashed potato.

"And witty as well." He chortled. "An utterly irresistible combination."

An urge to call him the old flirt he was washed over her, but she resisted the temptation. "I see you've brought our guests safely to us."

She scanned the group once again and spotted the man she assumed was Arnold's son, Rule Danforth. If he hadn't been deserted by his father thirty years ago, Rule would have grown up in extreme wealth. Mandy wondered what he was thinking now, and what he thought of the winner-take-all clause in Lydia's will.

His face was shaded by the broad brim of a black cowboy hat, but she scrutinized his shadowed features, trying to guess his mood. His profile was angular, stern, his heavy brows arched like hawk's wings spread in a dive for prey. His nose was lean and narrow, his lips nicely shaped, unsmiling above the square expanse of his jaw. All in all, his features presented a very pleasant image but no insight into his feelings.

Her glance roamed down. He was lanky and muscular. A white cotton sweater hugged his broad shoulders and chest. Rule Danforth looked like a man honed tough and strong by a rugged existence. He wore jeans that clung to trim hips and thighs, then tapered down over worn but polished boots. The jeans were not new, yet pressed and neat. It was obvious that Arnold Danforth's son worked hard for what he had and took care of it.

When Mandy's glance slid back to his face, his lips had lifted in a crooked smile. Curious about what had taken his fancy, she lifted her gaze to his eyes. They were deep set, an earthy brown, warm and distracting. And they were trained on her. A disturbing twinkle lit their depths. It was painfully clear that he was amused by her lingering tour of his body. Flustered, she looked away, riveting her attention on what Gavin Perth was saying.

"Meet Stephen Wrathmore, the son of Arnold's twin sister, Bessie."

The only other young man in the group stepped forward to grab Mandy's hand. He bore a strong resemblance to Rule, though he wasn't as tall. His hair was a medium brown and thinning, and he was dressed in a blue, button-down shirt with rose and bronze stripes, brown slacks and a loosened navy tie. A camera hung around his neck, giving him the look of a vacationing yuppie.

"How do you do, Mrs. McRae." His grip hurt. It was as though he'd decided if a weak grip made you a wimp, then a painful one must make you quite the opposite. She hid her grimace behind a polite smile.

"Nice batch of posies there. You grow 'em?" he asked.

"No, you dolt," came a guttural yet feminine voice.

Mandy felt Stephen's hand tighten on hers as he turned to face a tall, gaunt woman with cheekbones that were lethal weapons. She was the woman Mandy had originally thought to be a man.

"Oh...cow...poop!" Stephen defended himself haltingly, going petulant and red faced.

"Excellent comeback, Steppy, my boy. Next week we'll try something equally as pithy, such as, 'So's your mom.'"

Mandy's eyes widened at the put-down.

With an irritated "harrumph", the woman pushed Steppy's arm away and took Mandy's hand in a rather masculine grip of her own. "Ignore the child, my dear. Not only did Steppy get none of the business acumen of the family, he got very little of the brains—not to mention the hair. I'm Maybelle Poppy, dear departed Arnold's big sister." She lifted a bony hand and inhaled deeply on a pencil-thin cigar. "I adored that genius brother of mine," she added through a long exhale of smoke. "Did you know him?"

Unsettled by the woman's sharp tongue as well as her wild subject swing, Mandy stuttered, "No. I—I came here about a year after he died." She pulled out of the woman's grasp and moved her throbbing hand to the safety of her jeans pocket.

"No matter." Maybelle took a long drag. "By the by, in your work here, did you happen to notice any fresh mounds of dirt on the grounds? I mean, had Lydia been digging—"

"Wait a second," Steppy snapped. "No fair sneaking advance information."

"It doesn't matter, really," Mandy interjected. "I'm afraid I don't know a thing."

"Pity," Maybelle remarked tonelessly. "Well—I suppose I'll introduce you to my husband, Henry, anyway. His professional name is Skizzo the Great."

"'Skizzo the Geek,' she oughta say," Steppy snickered, lifting his camera and shooting Mandy and her basket. "Do you mind? Great composition."

She acquiesced with a weak smile, wondering what he'd meant by *geek*.

"You should talk, nephew," Maybelle groused hotly. "No one's ever accused you of being overly normal!"

"You know, Aunt Maybelle, on those rare occasions when your mouth's shut I can hardly tell you from the human beings."

Grinding out her cigar butt beneath her foot, she warned, "I'll deal with you later." Jerking around to scan the garden, she bellowed, "Oh, Skiiizzzzooo! Where are you, my noble droll?"

An elderly man peeked around a snowball hydrangea bush, a bowler hat tipped jauntily on his head. White flyaway hair stood out in disarray above his ears. Mandy stared in awe. He was the image of Elmer Fudd in an Einstein wig.

"Peek-a-boo, my little melon ball," came a singsong voice.

Melon ball? Mandy blinked. Was he kidding?

Henry Poppy waddled around the bush, revealing a paunchy body clad impeccably in a tweed suit and vest. He exhaled theatrically. "Ah, there's nothing better than an afternoon's cogitation to stimulate my brain cells."

"Except well-placed electrodes and a lightning storm," Steppy said in an aside.

Mandy glanced at him and then back at his aunt, wondering how she might react.

Maybelle shot Steppy a reproachful look as she helped her husband over a deep hedge of lavender but otherwise ignored him. "I'd like you to meet someone, Skizzo." She indicated Mandy, then lit a fresh cigarillo. "This is Mrs. McRae. She was Lydia's landscape architect."

Before Mandy realized what was happening, Henry Poppy had clutched her in a fatherly embrace, murmuring excitedly, "How Wanderlust! It's been ages!" He let go of her and shuffled back a step, beaming up at her from his five-foot-four-inch height. "You look exactly the same, my dear."

Mandy stared, dumbfounded. She'd never seen this man before in her life.

He reached into his vest pocket, pulled out a strip of cardboard and handed it to her. "Do be my guest at the matinee. I'm a clown, you know."

Mandy swallowed. "That's very—"

"A clown, you say?" Steppy interrupted, feigning shock. "And I always thought you were a rocket scientist for Barnum and Bailey. Go figure."

Mandy tried again. "Thank—"

"I wouldn't call someone else names, Mr.Blew-Daddy's-Car-Dealership-Fortune-in-Thirteen-Months Wrathmore!" Maybelle defended her husband amid a cloud of dark smoke. "Would you like me to fetch my whip to teach you some manners?"

"Whip . . . ?" Mandy echoed in an incredulous whisper. It was only when she heard Rule's chuckle that she realized she'd spoken out loud. She felt her cheeks grow warm and totally lost her train of thought.

"Ladies. Gentlemen. Please!" Mr. Perth held up his hands in a pleading gesture.

"You're very polite, young man." Henry placed a ticket in Mr. Perth's open hand. "Do attend the matinee as my guest. I'm Skizzo the Great, you know."

Mandy had tried unsuccessfully to break through to thank Henry Poppy for the ticket—blank and worthless though it was. She gave up, looking from Henry Poppy to his wife and then back in total astonishment. She'd heard that they were retired circus performers, but she hadn't heard that they were . . . well . . . bizarre.

"Thank you ever so much, Mr. Poppy," Mr. Perth remarked stiffly. He wadded the ticket into a ball at his side. Apparently Lydia's lawyer was uneasy with offbeat types. Lydia had been eccentric, but the Danforth family seemed destined for the *Guinness Book of World Records*.

"Lunch will be served shortly," Mr. Perth stated with crisp authority. "Mandy, I know you have to be getting back. Please, first, meet Jetta Poppy, Maybelle and Henry's daughter, and Rule Danforth, Arnold's son."

Mandy nodded to Jetta. The lovely, leggy redhead whom Mandy knew to be a Las Vegas dancer winked impishly. "You'll grow to love us, honey. Trust me."

Mandy recognized the kidding tone and smiled. Jetta Poppy sounded sane. Either she'd been adopted, or she'd had a very fortuitous dip into her parents' gene pool. "Hello, Jetta," she offered. "Call me Mandy."

Taking care to avoid Rule's amused eyes, Mandy turned to meet him, wondering if he were as nutty as he was good-looking.

She put her hand out tentatively, not sure anymore what a Danforth might do by way of greeting—crush the life out of her fingers, grab her bodily, or in Rule's case, maybe just smile her into a humiliated puddle.

She blanched inwardly at the foolishness of the thought and forced herself to look into his eyes. She just missed. At that second, a little girl pushed her way between two dwarf Japanese maples and grasped his thumb, drawing his attention. "Daddy? I'm hungry."

Prepared for almost any physical assault, Mandy was taken off her guard by the intrusion of a child incongruously dressed like a cowboy. She had the same black hair as her father and appeared to be about six years old. She clutched a worn, stuffed zebra to her chest.

The toy wore a crown of hybrid carnations, uniquely lovely with ruffled petals of lemon cream tipped in cobalt blue. Extremely rare, the carnations had cost Lydia a thousand dollars a plant. With wry amusement, Mandy calculated that the crown of blossoms was probably worth about four hundred dollars.

"What have you done, Dana?" Rule indicated the wilting petals. "This isn't your house. You mustn't pick flowers without permission."

Dana's face grew forlorn. "I'm sorry. . . ."

Mandy stepped closer and squatted beside the child. "Don't worry." She broke the stem off one of her silver roses and placed it behind Dana's ear. "You're a guest here. If you ever need flowers, just ask me. I'll show you where you can get all you want. Okay?"

Dana raised liquid green eyes to meet hers. A pang tore through Mandy's heart. It was amazing how much this little girl reminded her of her own Rebecca. She blinked back threatening tears and impulsively hugged the child. "Now you go have lunch," she managed in a ragged whisper. "We'll visit later."

When she stood, she glanced at Rule. There was gratitude in his eyes. It was such a compelling look that Mandy barely heard Mr. Perth's suggestion that the heirs go meet the house staff before luncheon.

Realizing that the group had begun to straggle toward the marble steps, she tugged her gaze away and started to turn to the kitchen entrance. Rule called after her. "Aren't you coming with us, Mrs. McRae?"

She smiled weakly. "I'm just a delivery boy around here. I live in a cottage on the hill."

"Does your husband work on the island, too?"

His question jarred her. She dropped her gaze and then returned it, realizing she would have to get used to questions like that when she left the island. "I—I'm a widow."

"I'm sorry," he murmured.

"It's been…two years." Her glance flitted around the solid cut of his jaw before she could will herself to look him in the eye. "I live with my father-in-law, Josh McRae. He's the caretaker here, but his health hasn't been too good since . . ." She realized she was rambling and looked away, feeling uneasy.

"He's a lucky man to have a loyal daughter-in-law like you."

His quiet remark made Mandy curious. She looked up. "What do you mean, like me?"

"Somebody who sticks around."

She sensed some dark emotion inside him, though his face was impassive.

Hoisting his daughter onto his shoulders, he changed the subject. "In your humble delivery boy's opinion, what do you think of the Danforth clan?"

She didn't quite know how to answer that, considering he was one of them.

A crooked grin softened his features. "Thinking of a polite synonym for *crazy*?"

She flushed. Could the man read minds? She decided he was guessing and fibbed. "Not at all. I'm sure they're very nice."

He arched a skeptical brow. "I can tell you don't lie often. You're not very good at it."

"This isn't fair." She laughed in spite of herself. "I've barely met your family."

"We're not exactly the Waltons, though, are we?"

"Yes we are!" Dana squealed. Mimicking John Boy in a grave little voice, she said, "G'night, ZeZe." She kissed her stuffed zebra with a loud smack. "G'night, Daddy." She patted his cheek with the relish of a schoolmarm.

"Ouch! Good night, you little bully." His brown eyes, full of laughter, never left Mandy as he added, "Good night, Mrs. McRae."

The intensity of that look gave her an odd feeling she couldn't quite name. With a shy smile, she played along. "Good night, Mr. Danforth."

She began to back down the path, unable to bring herself to turn away from those endearing brown eyes.

Something snagged her heel, and she found herself toppling over backward. She landed amid a spicy, scented bed of red flowers, her feet tangled in a border shrub.

Sputtering, she cleared her face of roses. "Oh, for Pete's sake!" she muttered, angry at her freak clumsiness.

"Are you all right?" Rule asked when she'd pushed herself up on her elbows.

She shook a stray leaf from her eyes.

"Where does it hurt?"

"No, no. I'm okay." She smiled feebly, feeling like an utter fool. "You probably won't believe me, but I never fall down."

His concerned expression eased, and he grinned. "I believe you, but to take care of any ugly gossip about you being clumsy, I'll pass the word that you're drunk."

She was unprepared for his remark. Unprepared for the dashing, teasing smile that lit his face. The hot embarrassment that had stained her cheeks drained away, and she found herself grinning back at him. "You'd do that for me?"

Rule's laughter was genuine and comforting. And nice to watch. But she had to get the roses to Emma, pronto. She turned to retrieve the scattered bouquet. "What exactly is it you do in New Mexico?" She surprised them both with the question.

"Daddy raises 'stinct horses," Dana supplied cheerfully.

"The word is *extinct*, sweetheart," Rule corrected.

He raises extinct horses? Mandy closed her eyes, feeling a little dejected. She should have known all the Danforths had been tarred with the same brush. It was a shame such a personable guy had to be as weird as his relatives. She turned back to her work, planning to escape as quickly as possible.

"Actually, the word's *endangered*, not *extinct*." Rule knelt beside her. "Not if I can help it, anyway. And they're relatives of horses."

"Endangered relatives of horses..." She hoped she could hide her skepticism. "Like what? Tall dogs?"

He chuckled. "Not exactly. Certain breeds of zebras, for example."

"Zebras?" There was a comforting solidarity about the word that sent a rush of relief through her. He must have seen a change in her expression because he gave a soft laugh. "You thought the Danforth curse had struck again, didn't you?"

"No...really..." She fumbled with a rose, dropping it twice.

"No problem. I just met the rest of them myself." As he spoke she turned to look at him. "My mother told me about them, though. They're about what I expected. Only more so."

Mandy was curious about his mother. Where was she? For that matter, where was his wife? She was suddenly very curious about this stranger. But since his life history wasn't her business, and she was late, anyway, she went back to her work. "Jetta seems nice," she offered as a neutral comment.

"Yes, she does. And I don't think Steppy would be half bad if he had a little self-confidence."

Pretty generous talk from a guy who might lose his inheritance to one of these people, Mandy thought. She wondered how she could have considered him anything but a nice, normal human being. "Tell me. How did you get into such an unusual occupation?"

He shook his head, and the grin he flashed her was disarming. "Long, boring story. Some rainy day when you have nothing to do, I'll put you to sleep with it."

When they both reached for the same rose, his hand grazed hers. It was warm, callused, strong. Mandy had the errant thought that he smelled awfully good, like clean sheets drying under sunshine and pine boughs. But there was an underlying scent. Pure male. Pure Rule Danforth. She inhaled, enjoying their casual intimacy.

"Daddy?" Dana interjected. "Is the lady done playing? Me and ZeZe's thirsty."

"ZeZe and I are thirsty."

"You are, Daddy? Want me ta get you handfuls of water from that little river over there?"

Rule's rich chuckle sent a pleasurable sensation to Mandy's nape. She touched the place and rubbed the tingle away.

"Never mind. We'd better go inside for that water." He turned to Mandy. "You'll be okay?"

"Sure." She stood and tossed him a careless grin. "I may be a reeling drunk, but I think I can make it to the kitchen."

"Can you forgive me for that remark?"

She laughed easily. "If you forgive me for thinking you were crazy."

"So you did think that." There was laughter in his eyes.

She shrugged and looked sheepish. "Maybe . . . a little."

"I don't blame you. There was plenty of circumstantial evidence."

"Friends?" Impulsively, she stuck out her hand.

He didn't just take her hand, he engulfed it. His grip was strong, but with a gentleness born of consideration, wholly unlike Steppy's. "Friends," he confirmed quietly.

That marvelous, amused glint in his eyes was difficult to turn away from, but she had learned the folly of walking backward in Rule Danforth's presence. Murmuring something about having to go, she drew her hand from the warmth of his and prudently pivoted, heading toward the kitchen at a brisk pace.

Rule watched her until she disappeared around the corner of the house. She was small boned and looked fragile. But she walked proudly, with the grace of a willow branch in a warm breeze.

He recalled the elfin scattering of freckles across her nose and sun-kissed cheeks, the thick, sandy-colored braid and the halo of loose wisps that framed her face. Her eyes were wide set, with dark blond lashes that surrounded irises so light blue that they almost took on the color of her silver roses. At one point he'd thought he'd seen sadness in their depths. He shrugged off the idea. It had probably just been the play of light and shadow across her face.

Mandy McRae seemed totally unaffected, either incapable or uninterested in pretending to be something she wasn't. Of course, appearances could be deceiving; he should know that by now.

"Daddy?" Dana broke through his thoughts, tugging on his belt.

"Okay, John Boy," he kidded, sweeping her up in his arms and striding up the mansion steps two at a time. "I know. You and ZeZe and the rest of the Waltons are thirsty."

Giggling, she said, "Oh, Daddy. You're funny." Laying a thin arm round his neck, she added, "I was gonna say, she's pretty."

"Who?"

"The flower lady. Don'tcha think?"

"I think..." He grew thoughtful for a moment. Mandy McRae was certainly pretty. But too many times it had been his experience that people, however great they seemed, were flawed and selfish underneath. He squeezed Dana. "I think, young lady, that pretty is as pretty does."

"What's that mean?"

Rule put Mandy from his thoughts and smiled at his daughter's wide-eyed curiosity. "That means that I think you're the prettiest lady in the whole wide world, when you're not picking other people's flowers."

As he pulled open the heavy door, Dana whispered into his neck, "I think you're pretty, too, Daddy."

2

"DON'T YOU love it, Mr. Danforth?" the young woman asked as she plopped down on the four-poster bed. "This embroidered linen spread was handmade in Denmark two hundred years ago."

"It's a great bedroom," Rule agreed, then added under his breath, "for Queen Victoria."

The blonde made a show of smoothing dark hose over a shapely leg. "By the way, may I call you Rule?"

"Sure." He smiled amicably.

"I hope you enjoyed the tour of the mansion." She sighed, sounding more breathless than fatigued. "This, of course, is your room."

"That's what I was afraid of," he said wryly but doubted that she'd heard him. She was too busy licking her fingers and smoothing her nylons.

"And that door leads through a bath to your daughter's room." She looked up as she massaged an ankle. "I hope you don't mind. I've been on my feet all day."

"Then it was especially kind of you to be my personal guide this afternoon, Miss DeWitt."

"Remember, it's Savina. And it's my pleasure," she cooed, her smile straight out of the coquette's handbook. "I was Lydia's personal secretary, you know. It's so sad, isn't it? That she's gone, I mean."

"I didn't know her," Rule said simply. It surprised him that Savina didn't know that Lydia was the woman his father had left him and his mother for thirty years ago, and therefore not a particularly cherished relative.

"Really?" Savina remarked, smoothing her chignon. Rule wondered idly if the platinum color was natural. He decided it was probably as real as the footlong lashes she'd been batting at him for the past hour.

She stood and removed a speck of lint from her short, body-hugging skirt. "My family isn't very close, either. Doesn't bother me a bit, though. Who needs them?" She walked toward him with a slither that would have done a sidewinder proud. "That little girl of yours dropped right off after lunch. She must have been really tired."

"Long trip."

"Oh, I know. You're from way out West."

"New Mex—"

"I love your boots." She hurried on, blithely unaware that he had tried to speak. "Do you have a hat? A cowboy hat, I mean?"

"I think so. A butler took it somewhere." He could smell her perfume now. It coiled about him, reminding him of overripe apples in the sun.

"Cowboys are sooo sexy, don't you think?" She lifted her chin and her breasts.

What the hell did she expect him to say? Unable to take her seriously, he agreed. "Incredibly sexy."

"Why, Rule, you're teasing me."

He half grinned at the depth of her insight. Lydia must have owed someone a big favor to have hired such a shallow creature as her secretary. Of course shallow didn't necessarily mean dumb. Savina had been reeling off history and descriptions of art objects and furniture all afternoon. No way was this woman dumb. Mercenary, yes. Self-centered, definitely. But she was no dummy.

"Did I mention that I was Lydia's secretary for nearly five years?"

"That long."

"Absolutely. And do you know what she left me for all that loyalty?"

"Can't say I do."

"Practically nothing, that's what. Do you think that's fair? I devoted five long years of my life to that nutty woman!"

Rule lifted a brow, but said nothing.

"I got to know her pretty well. The way she thought and all."

"I'm sure. Say, if the tour's over, I don't want to keep you . . ."

"I was thinking, Rule . . ." She allowed her lashes to flutter down, hiding the windows of her conniving little soul. "I could be a very . . . helpful partner in finding the treasure." She grazed his chest with hers. "If you get my meaning."

He cocked a brow in irritation. A potted plant could have gotten her meaning. She was as subtle as a neon sign flashing For Sale Cheap. He had an urge to haul her bodily from the room. But preferring to remain a gentleman if at all possible, he decided to give subtlety one more shot.

"Speaking of helpful, Savina, help me out here." He strode to the opposite corner of the room. A larger-than-life Roman marble torso caught his eye, and he tossed out conversationally, "Is this naked son of a gun supposed to be art, or is it just here to make me feel inadequate?"

After a long moment when she hadn't answered, he turned around. It was a fatal miscalculation. Savina's arms were instantly around his neck. She whispered huskily, "I have a feeling there's nothing inadequate about you . . ."

All he could see were shiny red lips, opened and coming toward him. He cursed inwardly.

"A fifty-fifty share, Rule. And you can have me. . . ." She pulled his face down, her lips finding his.

Fifty-fifty? Rule amended his opinion of her. The word *cheap* no longer applied.

Savina's kiss was fevered, as hard a sell as an overstocked used-car salesman might try—if open-mouthed kissing were allowed as a selling tool. Her arms curled around him like tentacles. She rubbed and twisted against him, making little pleasure noises in her throat. All in all, Savina's only effect on Rule was to turn him off completely.

His annoyance soaring, he disengaged himself from her as gently as his flaring temper would allow. When she realized he was drawing away, she grabbed for him. "Oh... Rule." Her voice faltered. He steadied her, holding her quivering body at bay. "Rule, darling..."

"Cut the crap, lady." His command was controlled but definite.

Her come-hither mask had crumbled. Now she was just a shaken young woman, who apparently thought something had gone on in their brief kiss that simply hadn't.

She wetted her trembling lips. "But, Rule...I.... Oh, the way you kiss!" Her voice was thick, unsteady.

"Stop it Savina," he growled. "This has gone far enough."

"You don't mean that." She reached for him again.

"Like hell, I don't." He corralled her arms, taking her by the wrists. "But I'll keep you in mind if I ever want a woman badly enough to pay for her." He took her elbow and propelled her toward the door. "Go cool off."

When he'd swung it open, she grabbed his arm, cutting with her long nails. In a snarl, she told him, "You don't deserve Lydia's money! You never even knew her or Arnold! Just who do you think you are, anyway?"

"Nobody special," he drawled, disgust twisting his lips. "Just Arnold Danforth's son, but don't let that impress you. It didn't impress him."

Her eyes brimmed with anger and humiliation as her nails bit deeper into his wrist. "It doesn't impress me, you big dumb cowboy! I'll show you. You'll be sorry you turned me down. Your brains are probably all in your pants, anyway!" She maliciously scraped his flesh as she released his arm. Choking back a sob, she hurried away, her stiletto heels hammering out an uneven retreat down the hall.

Fed up and tired, he closed the door and leaned heavily against it. After a minute, he looked up. Across the room he could see his scowling reflection in a gilt-edged mirror. "So, you big dumb cowboy," he muttered, rubbing his abused arm, "was it good for you?"

With a self-deprecating snort, he headed for the bathroom. He felt as if he needed a shower.

UNACCOUNTABLY RESTLESS, Mandy put away the last of the dinner dishes. She tossed the towel on its hook and walked out of the alcove that served as the cottage's kitchen. Her father-in-law was on the overstuffed couch, nestled in a crocheted coverlet, reading. In the meager lamplight, his face seemed gray, more fragile than usual. The parchment-fine skin looked shrunken and wasted, stretched thin over his hooked nose, pointed chin and jutting cheekbones.

Mandy smiled sympathetically at the old man. He'd seen more than his share of sadness and pain, yet his rheumy eyes glistened with strength and quiet humor. A bit wistfully, she asked, "How are you doing, Papa Josh?"

He peered at her over the rim of his reading glasses. His eyes were yellow and spidery with red veins. Sparse lashes narrowed as his features wrinkled more deeply in a slow smile. "'Bout the same as when you asked me ten minutes ago." His voice was weak and quavered with age. "I might ask the same question of you. You've been actin' like a hound on the scent of somethin' all evening."

"What an attractive analogy." She forced a laugh. Settling into a sagging chair, she gathered up the afghan she'd been crocheting. "Besides, I haven't acted any different than usual."

"Course not." He waved away the idea, his blue-veined hand quaking with palsy. "Y'always mop the floors and clean out the closets before ya whip up supper." He hiked a scrawny brow. "You sure there's nothin' you want to get off your chest?"

She tucked a foot beneath her. She knew she was squirming but unsure why. "I just felt like keeping busy."

There was a long silence as she crocheted. When she finally couldn't stand the suspense anymore she looked over at Josh. "What?" she asked suspiciously.

"Nothin'." His look was direct and kind. "Just wonderin' if any of those crazy relatives did anything to upset you?"

"Certainly not. I told you. Some of them are a little peculiar, but they aren't dangerous or anything. And I really like Rule."

"What about his little girl?"

Mandy lost a stitch. "What about her?"

"You said she reminded you of Rebecca." He paused. There'd been a tinge more quaver in his voice than could be blamed on his ill health. He pulled a big blue handkerchief from his shirt pocket and wiped his eyes.

Mandy let the crocheting sink into her lap. His small concession to grief pricked her heart. Rarely had he allowed her to witness it. How vulnerable he still was to the memory of his vivacious granddaughter.

When he stuffed the handkerchief back in his pocket, he asked a bit more steadily, "That what's botherin' you?"

Her gaze dipped to the rag rug. "I guess seeing Dana started me thinking. Rebecca would have been almost her age now. I couldn't help wondering what Rebecca would have been like if she'd . . ."

"She'd've been as beautiful as her mother," he remarked almost too softly to hear.

Mandy's lips lifted tremulously. It was a great comfort to have Josh around—someone who could talk about Rebecca, who could remember with her. He deserved so much better than he'd gotten from life—first losing his wife, then his only son and granddaughter. She desperately wished there was something she could do to make his life easier, happier. In a spontaneous urge to show him how much he had come to mean to her in these past two years, she pushed out of the deep chair and walked over to him. "Rebecca loved you very much."

Dropping to her knees, she hugged his frail shoulders. "I do, too. You've helped me through so much, Papa Josh."

His breathing made shallow wheezing sounds near her ear as he patted her shoulder. "You've been a better daughter to me than most blood kin could boast, Mandy. You're the blessin', not me."

She pulled his sweater more securely around his shoulders, whispering unsteadily, "Thanks." When she kissed his cool cheek she could taste a salty dampness. She swallowed, wanting to cry out. Wanting to do something to help him. How could Lydia have been so thoughtless? She balled her fists, angry for one more countless time since the will had been read.

Frothy sheers at the window billowed out, beckoning for their attention. Josh indicated them with shaky fingers. "Softest night so far this summer. Smells the way I remember my Minna's dressing table always smelled. Sweet and sorta comfy."

Mandy inhaled deeply of the lavender-drenched breeze wafting in. "It is lovely."

"Why don't you take a little walk? Do you good."

She gazed at him fondly, her anger draining away. "You wouldn't mind?"

He took off his glasses and waggled them at her. "Shoo, now. It'll give me some relief from that noisy crochet hook clackin' all evening."

"Noisy crochet hook, indeed." She kissed his forehead as she stood. He had changed the subject trying to lighten the mood and Mandy was grateful. Dwelling on the past would do neither of them any good.

She walked to the closet and pulled out a navy sweater, slipping it on over her navy oxford shirt. "See you later." On her way out the door, she blew him a kiss.

He replaced his glasses and nodded. As she closed the door, she could see him reaching for his handkerchief. A shaft of sorrow shot through her. She cursed Lydia's lack of foresight, wishing there was something she could do to mend the sad situation Lydia's will would soon force upon Josh.

She closed the door behind her and inhaled deeply of dampness, brine and a harmony of floral scents. Striking out aimlessly, she headed away from the cottage along the cliff. Walking over the windswept crags of Barren Heath Isle helped ease the tug at her heart.

Two years had gone by since she'd lost Peter and Rebecca. She'd thought she had put most of that pain behind her, but seeing little Dana today had brought back a flood of memories.

Stuffing her hands into her slacks pockets, she wandered, directionless, for over an hour. Nature's diverse perfection helped ease her restless soul.

After some star gazing, she found herself heading toward the bride's garden, her private haven. Within a high circular wall, the little bower held, for Mandy, the tranquillity of an old convent garden. Trouble seemed to stop at its gate.

She entered a grove of weeping beeches and approached the garden along a stone path. Even from this distance, the silver roses, ferns and an infinity of white-blooming perennials laced the night air with innocent sweetness.

Her hand was poised over the gate's latch when she heard voices. One was unmistakably Rule's, but to whom was he speaking? Hesitating, she stood on tiptoe and peered over the gate. Rule's features, caught there between heaven's light and earth's darkness, were more sharply chiseled than she remembered. He stood not quite facing her. Beside him was an eighteenth-century bloodstone fountain, the garden's centerpiece. A spray of water gurgled and spiraled from it, reflecting the full moon in a hundred cascading rivulets.

Dana was sitting on the fountain's edge, trailing a finger in the water. She clutched her stuffed zebra.

Except for an added denim jacket, Dana was dressed as she had been when they'd arrived—western shirt, crisp new jeans and a pair of tiny cowboy boots. Her tomboy clothes seemed at odds with her delicate frame. Of course, Mandy couldn't see Rule in a frilly little girls' department. She smiled at the improbable image of him sorting through racks of lace and ruffles.

Mandy wondered about Dana's mother. Surely she shopped for her daughter. But Dana's appearance didn't suggest a woman's touch. She wondered why.

She recalled the trunk with bolts of pastel fabrics she'd put away after Rebecca's death and her smile faded. Maybe she could make Dana something feminine and frilly while she was on the island. A little girl could always use a new dress.

"But why did we come here to play a game, Daddy? It seems silly," Dana asked, interrupting Mandy's thoughts.

Rule chuckled. "Out of the mouths of babes."

"What, Daddy?"

"I think it's pretty silly, too, but the prize to be won is very big."

She stopped trailing her finger and looked up, wide-eyed. "Big like a car?"

Rule turned to stare out over the ocean. "More like a home."

"A house? But we have a house, Daddy."

"Only till the end of the summer. Then a big company is going to build a factory on the land we've been leasing."

"What's leasing?"

"Sort of like borrowing."

"Oh." She frowned. "What'll happen to Big Mac and Tuffie and Clipper and all the rest?"

He turned back and tousled her hair. "If we find the prize, our zebras and horses can come here. Then they can have babies of their own who will grow up strong with our help, and they won't become extinct. I've told you about what happens when something becomes extinct."

She screwed up her face in thought. "Oh, yes. They'll disappear."

"In a way. We wouldn't want that, would we?"

"No. We wouldn't! We must find the treasure, Daddy!" Coming up on her knees, she hugged his middle. "You can do it, Daddy. Daddy?"

He put his arms around her. "Yes, Dana?"

"Is Mommy x-tinct?"

Even from the place where Mandy stood, she could see Rule stiffen. "No..." he whispered. "Mommy went away."

"Then she'll come back?"

"I've told you, no."

"Oh, yeah. Mommy divided us." She sighed. "I forgot."

"Divorced. And you didn't forget. Now, enough talk. Off to bed." He swept her up in his arms, and she giggled with delight as he strode toward the gate.

Realizing she was about to be caught in first-degree eavesdropping, Mandy felt a flicker of panic. Stumbling on an uneven stone, she fell with a thud. A vise of pain crushed her ribs, forcing all the air from her lungs. The gate swung open, hiding her from Rule's view.

She could do nothing but lie there in agony as his footfalls grew distant along the stone walkway. She winced, but didn't have the breath to call for help. Even if she had, she would have chosen to suffer in silence rather than have Rule know she had been lurking in the darkness, listening.

After a moment, she sucked in a shaky breath and decided she was going to live. She felt ashamed of herself for her childishness and wanted to get back to the cottage and forget this ever happened. She started to stand, but a sharp pain in her hip forced her to drop back down. Squelching a groan, she felt around in the darkness until she came up with a rock the size of an egg. She eyed it with distaste, turning it in her fingers.

"Justice in action," she muttered. Tossing the rock away, she leaned against the cold stone wall. Trying but failing to force the throbbing in her hip from her mind, she mulled over the conversation she'd overheard. Rule needed Barren Heath Isle for endangered animals. In her wildest imaginings, she couldn't think of a more unselfish use for the island.

Drawing her lower lip between her teeth, she began to scrape together an idea—a rash plan that might not only help Rule get a home for his animals, but also help Papa Josh. It was exactly the chance she'd been praying for. She sat in the shadows for a long time, trying to work out the best way to present her scheme to Rule so that he wouldn't be able to turn her down.

EMMA, THE ELDERLY COOK, had taken charge of Dana, feeding her freshly baked cookies and promising to get her into a warm bath. Needing some time to himself, Rule walked out onto the mansion's front gallery. The wind had picked up high on the bluff, and he could hear its howl as it slashed through lofty branches.

He felt impatient. Inhaling the crisp June night, he leaned wearily on a cold pillar and worked at eliminating Savina's perfume from his nostrils. How could she have believed that he would agree to her offer— under the nose of his own daughter?

It wasn't that he hadn't enjoyed women since his wife had walked out. He'd taken advantage of situations that had been mutually agreeable and discreet. Life had taught him that relationships were fragile and impermanent at best, so he'd learned to avoid them for less binding affairs. Even so, Savina's proposition had been so cold-blooded that Rule couldn't muster enough respect for her to accept her deal—even on a purely business basis, let alone work up any desire for her body.

He found his thoughts drifting to Mandy McRae. He recalled her subtle scent, her lush voice and those silver eyes, vibrant, yet vulnerable. They reminded him of the silver roses in the garden not far away.

Deciding to walk, he drifted down the marble steps and roved through the formal gardens. Going nowhere in particular, he followed a stone path that led toward the walled garden where he and Dana had been moments before.

When he was a few steps from the gate, he noticed movement in the shadows and stopped short, alert. He was surprised to see Mandy sitting in the grass, leaning against the wall. "What the—"

"Oh, Rule." She sat up abruptly, her expression both surprised and guilty. "I didn't hear you coming."

"Are you all right?" He leaned down to offer her a hand.

Mandy accepted his help up. "I'm fine. Just stumbled and was catching my breath."

"You're sure you're okay?"

"I'm fine, honestly." She cast him a sidelong glance, wondering how solicitous he would be if he knew why she'd fallen. She faked nonchalance. "Rule, I'm glad you happened by. Would you walk with me for a minute? In the bride's garden?"

He gave her a steady look. "If you like."

She glanced around, taking in the deserted grounds. Confident that they were alone, she preceded him through the gate.

"This is my favorite place," she remarked as he came up beside her. "It's the silver roses. They're unique."

"Like your eyes."

Mandy's gaze lifted in surprise, and he smiled. "Your eyes are a very unusual color. I noticed them this afternoon."

"Oh . . ." With his simple observation her wits scattered like leaves in a high wind. She picked a rose to fill the time it took her to gather them. "Thank you. The roses are a rare hybrid. The Sterling Goddess is the most costly rose in the world."

"You designed this garden, didn't you?"

"Yes." She held the rose up and inhaled, watching him surreptitiously over the petals. He seemed to be studying her, and she had the wild notion he was trying to read her motives for inviting him out here.

"Naturally, there were gardens here before I came, but they were overgrown and in ill repair. I thought this knoll of weeping beeches cried out for an intimate garden."

"Is it called a bride's garden because of the white flowers or because it would be a picturesque setting for a wedding?"

"A little of both." Mandy moved to lean against the fountain. "You're very perceptive."

"It wouldn't take a mental giant to figure that out."

Her laughter was stiff. This attempt at small talk was making her nervous. She needed to get to the point. Taking a deep breath, she gazed out over the water that glistened in the distance. The wind had picked up, ruffling her hair. High on the bluff, she could hear its mournful whine in the branches of the pines and cypress beyond Josh's cottage.

She'd grown to love the sounds and scents, the wind-scarred cliffs, the brilliance and fog of Barren Heath Isle. She loved the sharp clarity of its crashing waves and shrieking winds, the mystery of its caves and woods, the fragrant fields of wildflowers and grasses that stretched on for hundreds of acres.

Mandy had been on the island for less than two years. Papa Josh had been there more than forty. What cruelty to make him leave it now.

She pressed her trembling hands together, willing herself to be calm. She was a proud woman, unused to asking favors of strangers. She wasn't quite sure how she was going to go about this. All she knew was that if she was going to do anything, it had to be now. The hunt was to begin in the morning.

When she turned back, Rule was looking at her. He seemed to be waiting for her to ask him something.

She smiled at him, hoping her voice wouldn't crack and give away her nervousness. "Rule, I've been thinking about the treasure hunt." The moon suddenly disappeared behind a cloud, and she was forced to move closer to better judge his reaction. "I could help you."

They were so close now that she could see the fractional lift of his brow.

"We could help each other." She added hopefully. "I have a—"

"Proposition for me," he finished flatly.

She blinked in surprise. "How did you know?"

"Just a guess."

The moon had slipped quickly back, as though titillated by their conversation and interested in hearing more. Mandy could see Rule's jaw work angrily and she frowned, puzzled. His gaze had gone brooding, and he seemed to be fighting some internal battle.

What had she said to upset him? "Rule, if you hear me out, I promise you won't regret—"

"I've already heard the pitch," he bit out. "Let's see what you've got to trade." His arms went around her, pulling her to him.

She sucked in a startled breath as he lowered his lips to hers. His kiss was soft and slow, completely at odds with the flash of contempt she had seen in his eyes an instant before. His mouth moved over hers in a lazy seduction, and his strong, seeking fingers ran up her back to her nape, massaging, weaving a fiery spell.

It had been a very long time since Mandy had known the powerful arms of a man around her or the subtle stroke of knowing hands. Her body quivered, instinctively understanding that he would be a sublime lover.

Sensing her reaction, Rule drew her closer until their bodies were molded together. Mandy fought a tremor of need that was flaming to life deep inside her. The wind howled like a banshee, and a wave crashed with the might of a thousand stones against the sea wall. But the thundering and keening of nature surrounding them was no match for the din of Mandy's emotions.

She clutched at him, frightened, as his lips took a long, spellbinding journey over her face. She was floundering, drowning in a sea of primitive sensations that she'd thought she'd put aside. The relentless surge of desire that was overwhelming her left her dazed, yet too ravenous to push him away.

Rule traced the lobe of her ear with his tongue, whispering, "Sleeping with you would be worth a fortune."

Breathing jerkily, Mandy pulled away from him and stared. She felt weak. Everything was out of focus.

"Just how much of the inheritance do you want for your sex?" Rule asked, his voice rough with passion.

"For my . . . sex?" Mandy repeated, feeling stuporous. Finally, in a searing flash, she absorbed his words.

Struggling from his grasp, she stumbled backwards against the fountain. "Why you conceited . . . *worm!*"

Something flashed in his eyes, but she couldn't tell if it was annoyance or surprise.

"How could you think that I-I would . . . Ooooooh, *never mind!*" She spun wildly away. "I was totally wrong about you! Good night, Mr. Danforth."

3

As she marched to the gate, her back was so stiff with righteous indignation that he could almost believe she was actually incensed, that she had never intended to offer what Savina had so recently and blatantly suggested. He was highly skeptical that he could have been so wrong about her motives, but he was too intrigued to let her run off into the night without another word.

She'd kissed him with the potency of a siren. He'd always thought they were purely mythical beings with the sexual allure to cause ships to break up on the rocks. But now he wasn't so sure they were so mythical. He had to admit that at least part of his body felt a little shipwrecked at the moment.

He frowned in memory. After the kiss had ended, she'd quivered and retreated like a wounded virgin. What was her story, anyway?

"Mandy?" Rule's voice had gone quiet, more curious now than irritated.

The change was so unexpected that she couldn't keep herself from turning back. "What?" she snapped. Even in her embarrassment and fury, she noticed that the grimness had faded from around his mouth.

He pursed his lips, raking her stone-stiff form with doubtful eyes. "What the hell is going on here?"

"I'll tell you what," she lashed back. "You just made a complete ass of yourself."

"Are you saying I misunderstood your offer?"

"Misunderstood!" She scoffed hotly. "Do ever-blooming violas bloom all summer?"

"Damned if I know," he muttered, closing the distance between them in three long strides. "Damned if I know what we're talking about."

"You might try listening."

Crossing his arms casually across his chest, he suggested quietly, "Talk. I'll do nothing but listen this time."

She jerked around to face the ocean. She was in pain because of her intense reaction to his kiss. It had bothered her much more than she'd imagined a simple little kiss could. After a tense moment, she felt steady enough to speak. "I know the island, Rule. I could help you find Lydia's fortune. All I ask is that, if you win, you allow Papa Josh to live out his life here, in his cottage, and make sure he's well cared for."

The wind had died, and all Mandy could hear was the wild tripping of her own heartbeat.

Rule kept silent for a long moment. Finally he asked, "Didn't Lydia provide for him in her will?"

"A small pension, but don't you see?" She turned back, imploring. "That cottage has been his home for a very long time. He's not well, and I'm afraid he won't survive if he's forced to leave Barren Heath Isle."

"What about you?"

"I had a career before I came here. I've put out feelers."

He was watching her with eyes that could only be described as disarming. She swallowed hard. It was no easy task to maintain eye contact with this man. He exuded the most exasperating charm. "What—" Her voice cracked. Clearing her throat, she tried again. "What do you say to my proposition?"

"I don't believe you." Though spoken softly, his words had a suffocating effect on her, and she blanched. She forced herself to look directly into his eyes.

"I see . . ." With a stiff back, she turned toward the gate. She would not beg.

"Are you for real?" Rule's voice halted her.

"What do you mean?" she asked very quietly.

"I mean, if you're serious about helping me for Josh's sake . . ."

Mandy closed her eyes, hoping against hope that his next words would be the ones she needed to hear.

It was deathly quiet and time dragged by. She'd about given up hope when Rule said simply, "I accept."

Grabbing a steadying breath, she spoke through it. "Thank you. . . ."

"Mandy—"

"I'm very grateful to you," she cut in abruptly. "Good night." She knew she should have turned back. He deserved a handshake at least, even a hug. But something deep inside her was still reeling from the last time he'd touched her . . . kissed her. She didn't have the strength even to turn and face him right now. Her emotions were hanging in tatters around her like a coat that could no longer keep out the cold. Hurrying away, she murmured, "Come to the cottage after breakfast."

The gate clattered shut behind her and she fled to the cabin. Rushing to her room, she flung herself across her bed and stared at the ceiling, feeling numb.

The hard delight of his body against hers had taken a heavy toll. She hadn't been caressed by another man since she'd met Peter. And suddenly, tonight, she had found herself hungering for a virtual stranger.

She hugged herself and shivered, wishing she had never gone for a walk tonight—wishing that the memory of Rule's kiss, his hands, the slight roughness of his

cheek, hadn't sent waves of long-buried desire cours-
ing through her.

Peter had been her love. Peter, sweet Peter. They'd
met and married her junior year in college. He was ten
years her senior and a commercial airplane pilot.

Mandy recalled how happy Peter had been eight
years later when he'd been able to afford his own small
plane. He'd planned to take Mandy and Rebecca up that
afternoon. Mandy had been forced to cancel owing to
some work that had come up unexpectedly.

Peter decided not to disappoint Rebecca. It would be
their daughter's first flight. She remembered Peter taking her into his arms before he left, saying, "Love me,
Mandy?" He always said that before he left on a flight.

Mandy always kissed him and said, "Forever and
ever, darling."

Then Peter would smile and touch her nose. "I'll hold
you to that." It was a ritual they never deviated from.
They both believed it was their good-luck charm.

She wiped away a lone tear with the back of her
hand. As long as she kept Peter and Rebecca alive with
her love, they could never really be gone. "Forever and
ever, darling," she whispered. Yet every time she tried
to picture Peter in her mind, why could she see only
Rule's eyes beckoning, Rule's lips taunting? Why did the
fragrant night have to drag by on lumbering feet, while
sleep denied her the refuge of oblivion?

RULE LOOKED AROUND the opulent dining room. At one
end the light of a log fire reflected in a well-polished
marble floor. Savina was prattling that the stenciled
wallpaper, a soft orange and green, was based on an
Oriental Bukhara embroidery. A swollen little chest
with ornate inlay, called a Venetian commode, stood
at the entrance to the pantry. It was covered with silver

serving dishes now holding little more than drippings and crumbs.

The chandelier, hanging almost low enough to skim the rosewood table, was of Dresden porcelain. It was six tiers of white china that spanned out to a four-foot diameter. Each tier supported a group of electrically flickering candles. The room was dark for eight o'clock in the morning. Though there were three floor-to-ceiling windows in the room, their green velvet drapes were open only a crack.

Rule closed his eyes, wishing he were back in his sunny ranch house kitchen where the food was served right from the stove onto a sturdy, if inelegant, table. His crusty old cook knew how to birth a breach colt with one beefy fist while he scrambled eggs fit for angels with the other.

"Well, I just have one thing on my mind this morning." Steppy rubbed his hands together in anticipation.

"That's one more than usual," Maybelle remarked archly, blowing a ring of smoke across the table.

"You know, Auntie dearest, I can't wait till they come out with a really big can of bug spray."

Maybelle crushed out her cigar in his croissant. "That's just the sort of remark I'd expect from a man with jelly on his tie."

Savina wet her napkin in her water glass and began to wipe the spot, whispering to him under her breath. Rule noticed with mild interest that she was sitting next to Steppy this morning. Apparently a bargain had been struck between them last night.

"Mother, Steppy, really. We're guests." Jetta Poppy was sitting on Rule's right. Her profile was beautiful even in a frown. She reached around the corner of the table and touched Mr. Perth familiarly on the hand.

"The natives are restless, Gavin. Isn't it about time for our first clue?"

Rule raised a brow. First names already? Was Jetta another angling female? His thoughts turned back to Mandy's proposition the evening before. He'd mistrusted her and treated her shabbily. He'd had most of the night to berate himself for it, and he'd slept hardly at all. But as morning dawned, Rule's gut had begun to gnaw with pesky doubts. Were Mandy's motives as pure as they had seemed, or had her kiss affected his reasoning?

Now, looking around, he'd begun to have serious doubts. Was Mandy really any different from Jetta or Savina? He stabbed repeatedly at his apple brown Betty, his thoughts growing dark and suspicious.

Highly irritated with himself, he dropped his fork, grimly resolving to take Mandy at her word. Just because life had made him reluctant to trust people, didn't mean Mandy had secret, selfish motives behind her offer to help him. He was probably just overtired and allowing his imagination to run wild. Nevertheless, an irritating inner voice seemed to delight in reminding him, *Time will tell what Mandy's real motives are.*

Clearing his throat, Gavin Perth stood. He pulled at his goatee and smiled broadly. "My friends, as you know the time has come to begin the hunt." He drew an envelope from his breast pocket and opened it with a flourish.

Rule sat back, crossed his arms in an effort to relax and thought once again of Mandy. Her small form had molded to him so eagerly, yet she had trembled like a terrified bird.

Mr. Perth coughed, drawing Rule back. It surprised him that his thoughts had wandered so flagrantly when his future and the future of his endangered equines rested on what Mr. Perth was about to say.

"The first clue is 'A square within a circle.'" Mr. Perth looked up, his expression as puzzled as the guests'.

"What the hell does that mean?" Steppy shouted.

"Elementary my dear Wattage," Henry Poppy sang out.

"Oh, sure," Steppy laughed snidely. "The man with the intellect of a poached egg has it figured out. What is it, Unk? I'm all atwitter."

Henry hoisted himself up and reached across the table. "So glad to meet you, Mr. Twitter. I'm Skizzo the Great. Please be my guest at the matinee." He handed his glowering nephew a ticket and sat back down.

"Mr. Twitter," Steppy muttered, rolling his eyes in divine agony.

"May I continue, Mr. Wrathmore?" Gavin Perth inquired frostily.

Steppy grunted and dropped the ticket in his cold coffee.

"As I was saying, the rules specify, no disfiguring or dismantling of the mansion itself. You may dig on the grounds, but avoid the gardens. There will be absolutely no digging inside the gardens. Is that understood?"

There was a collective nod.

"In that case, please feel free to begin the hunt."

The party broke up with all the style and grace of a Keystone Cops car chase. Steppy and Savina bolted out the door, followed shortly by Maybelle, dragging her merry little husband in her wake. Mr. Perth popped a final piece of cheese pastry in his mouth and sauntered off down the hall.

Jetta stood, smoothing her sequined sweater. Its neckline was cut low enough to reveal a splendid cleavage. She ran long fingers through her hellcat hair and sighed expansively. "Nothing like a family reunion to make you remember why you ran away from home." She toyed with Rule's butter knife absently. "Aren't my parents the quaintest couple? Imagine my girlhood—Mama in her helmet, smoking her black cigars, and Skizzo the Red-Nosed Nitwit...."

"Hardly a Norman Rockwell painting," Rule remarked with a crooked grin.

She laughed without humor. "Oh, well, enough about my idyllic girlhood." She waved away the subject with a heavily jeweled hand. "'A square within a circle' is some clue. Sounds like the lunks I date. Square pegs in round holes abound in Las Vegas."

She smiled, her large red lips opening to expose perfect teeth. "What about you? Aren't you going to join the mad dash?"

He sat forward and took a last sip of his water from a dainty cut-glass goblet that felt foreign in his large hand. "Think I'll let the dust settle first."

"What do you figure the clue means?" she asked.

Rule grinned up at her. "Sounds like the way I feel in this mansion—very square. I'm used to humbler circumstances."

"A hunk like you fits in anywhere. And as for women, I'll bet all you have to do is smile that innocent smile and say 'Howdy, ma'am'." She winked. "Gets 'em every time. Am I right?"

Rule chuckled at her forthrightness. "But not you, I'll wager."

She winked again, an affectation she seemed quite fond of. "You got it, cousin. I know men, and for the most part, I don't like what I know." She winked. "No offense."

He laughed. "None taken."

She put her hands on slender hips. "I'm thirty-three years old. I've been a dancer for almost fifteen years, and believe me, I'm dying to get away from liniment and hot lights. Not to mention the eternal dieting."

He put his glass down and asked, "What would you do with the money if you got it?"

She lifted a shoulder in a sexy shrug. "I've got my eye on a piece of resort property that's just begging for development. If I dig up Lydia's bucks, I, for once, will be in control, instead of every egotistical man I've ever met. You know, I think that old broad would love it if I found her fortune. What do you think?"

He unfolded his lanky body from the chair, still smiling at her. "I wouldn't attempt to guess what any woman wants."

"Very wise." The wink flashed again.

It must have been catching. He almost winked back. Rule decided he liked the outspoken, tough lady. "Good luck, Jetta."

"Break a leg." Her thick, honeyed laugh lingered behind her as she swung languidly down the hall.

Dana had eaten breakfast in the kitchen. Retrieving her, Rule headed for the cottage where he could see a pale, elderly man slumped on a porch swing. "Hello, there," Rule called.

Seeming to come awake, the man lifted a hand. It shook so badly that he almost dropped his pipe. "'Lo!" He beckoned. "Been hopin' I'd get a chance to meet some of the relatives." He tapped his chest with a bony finger. "Bad ticker. Don't get around much anymore." He put out a creased and quivering hand. "You must be the son. I'm Joshua McRae. Call me Josh."

Rule took the weathered hand in his. It felt cold and dry, but the fingers clung with the dregs of what once had been a hearty strength. "Good to meet you, Josh. I'm Rule Danforth."

Josh nodded approvingly, squinting first up and then down Rule's six-foot-five-inch frame. "Your papa was a big man, too, but he didn't have the muscle you've got."

Rule's smile was melancholy. "He probably didn't lift that many hundred-pound sacks of feed."

"Not so I ever noticed." His chuckle was feeble. "What's that name, again?"

"Rule."

"Like it. Has a good, strong sound." Josh squinted down at the small girl who stood behind her father's leg. His old eyes seemed to cloud over for an instant, but he quickly recovered, his face creasing in a smile. "And who might this be—a wood nymph come to dance away the dew?"

Dana's brows knit and she looked up at her father. Rule only smiled.

Dana looked back. "What's that mean?"

Josh beckoned for her to come sit beside him. "Say, little one, you're mighty pretty. Tell me your name and I'll tell you about the dance of the wood nymphs. How's that?"

With an encouraging nod from her father, Dana crawled up beside the old man, hugging her stuffed zebra protectively in front of her.

"Is Mandy around?" Rule asked.

Josh looked up, surprised. "Why, yes. She's down in the meadow yonder." He frowned in question. "You want to see her?"

"Yes, if it's all right."

Josh looked doubtful. "It's all right by me, son, but I dunno if you'll feel the same when you get there. Mandy's a fine person, but she's got herself one bedevilin' flaw." He motioned beyond the cabin. "Before the woods, take the path that meanders down. You'll find her soon enough."

"Thanks." Rule grew concerned. He'd thought they'd parted on fairly good terms, considering everything. Had he been wrong?

"Daddy," Dana called. "Where are you going?"

Rule turned, but Josh patted the girl's head. "Now about those wood nymphs. Do you know they're only two inches tall?"

Dana turned back, wide-eyed. "Aw, you're kidding."

With Josh's enfeebled laugh, Rule smiled and walked off to find Mandy. He wondered what her mood would be when he found her.

He followed the path until it wound down into a valley dotted with buttercups, daisies and purple clover. A breeze touched the grasses, making them sway and bow before him. As he walked, he heard the squawk of a crow, or was it the screech of an angry bluejay? An instant later he heard the plaintive howl of a dog. He wondered if a baby bird had fallen from its nest, and the mother was fighting to save it from the animal.

Rounding a stand of red maples, Rule came to a riveted halt, shocked—not by nature in cruel havoc—but by Mandy, sawing away on a violin. An old hound was squatting beside her, moaning, his muzzle thrown toward the sky in either agony or ecstasy. It was hard to tell.

Mandy was turned slightly away from Rule, her slender form half hidden in the grass and bright flowers. She appeared much like a flower herself in a pink, oversize shirt and snug jeans.

A large basket sat on the ground beside her. It was filled with blossoms. Rule enjoyed a pleasant view of her hips as she bent to dodge an amorous bee, but he winced at the squawk from the instrument when her bow slid sideways across the strings.

Shiny tendrils of hair had escaped her braid and danced around her face. Her profile was serious as she concentrated on sheet music clothespinned to a low branch. She looked charming standing there murdering the piece of music. Somehow, seeing her like that, he couldn't imagine her with anything but the most innocent of motives. Feeling stupid that he'd ever doubted her, he called out, "Hi, there, partner."

Mandy's recital scraped to a halt. The hound scampered away as she whirled to see Rule's broad wave. "Oh—it's you," she gasped, her cheeks flushing. "I didn't expect you for another half hour." She seemed embarrassed at being interrupted. He smiled encouragingly, indicating the violin. "Just beginning?"

She knelt to place the violin in its case. "I've played all my life, much to my family's dismay. It relaxes me." She snapped the case shut. "Emma's cats hide in the attic, but old Rosco seems to enjoy it."

Rule fought the urge to chuckle. "I could see that."

She stood, taking the music down from the branch. Folding it, she stuck it in her hip pocket. "I gather you're here with the clue?"

"Yes, such as it is. But I'd like to know more about your music."

She smiled uneasily, "I'll let you know when my next concert is. There'll be standing room only in the attic."

"That won't affect me." His smile broadened. "I'm like Rosco. More the howling type."

A flicker of surprise flitted across her face. An instant later, her cheeks flushed scarlet. It was a completely unexpected, completely charming reaction to his casual remark, and he wondered why it had embarrassed her.

She cleared her throat and changed the subject. "So, what's the clue?"

"Okay." He shrugged. "Does 'a square within a circle' give you any hot ideas?"

Mandy's brows knitted. "It isn't much, is it?"

Rule spotted an outcropping of rock and motioned toward it. "Why don't we sit?"

Picking up Mandy's basket and her violin case, he followed her to the stones where she perched on one hip. He took a seat beside her but didn't speak, allowing her time to think.

"Well, there's the bride's garden, but the fountain in the center is round, so—"

"Mandy," Rule interrupted, needing to know once and for all. "Why did you come to me with your offer rather than one of the others?"

She shifted her gaze to him. "Because you need a home for your endangered—" She stopped abruptly as his eyes narrowed.

"How do you know about that?"

She realized her slip too late. She could only have known about it because she'd been eavesdropping. Her gaze slid to her hands as she admitted, "I happened to overhear you talking to Dana in the bride's garden. I had no right to listen to your conversation, I know." She stuttered, "I—I didn't realize I was eavesdropping until you started for the gate. I was so ashamed that I panicked and fell."

"That's what you were doing on the ground?"

"Yes." She forced herself to look at him and spread her hands apologetically. "I was recuperating from my crime spree. I couldn't breathe for five minutes. There's a bruise on my hip the size of a potato, if that's any consolation."

Rule managed to suppress a grin, but he couldn't suppress the urge to cup her chin in his fingers. "I've given you some pretty bad moments in the past twenty-four hours, haven't I?"

Her lashes dipped, hiding her eyes from his slow perusal. She remained silent.

"You forgave me for the stupid kiss last night. I think I can forgive a little unpremeditated eavesdropping." He paused. "You did forgive me, didn't you?"

"Of course," she whispered, feeling a sliver of heat through her at the memory. "It's totally forgotten," she lied. Wary of the power of his touch, she shifted away, wincing with the pain in her hip.

"That really hurts, doesn't it." Rule scrutinized her lower anatomy with a thoroughness that made Mandy's pulse race. "Did you put ice on it?"

"I didn't notice it until this morning."

He took her hand and helped her to her feet. "Then we'll do it now."

"We?" she gasped, pulling her fingers from his grasp. "I don't think so."

He chuckled. "My Somali wild asses are boisterous and get injured a lot. I treat them."

Mandy peered at him narrowly. His eyes were quite appealing when he smiled. Too appealing. She took a deliberate step back. "I'm sure you're wonderful with wild asses, but you're not touching my wild . . . my hip with ice or with anything else." She bit her lip, not pleased with the way that had come out.

Unruffled, Rule gathered up her basket for her. "All right. You put the ice on your hip while you think of places the clue might refer to and I'll rustle up an early lunch. That breakfast this morning was a little frilly for my taste."

"I really don't—"

"Trust me." His dark eyes glittered with good humor.

She cocked her head in speculation. "How many unsuspecting females per week fall prey to that innocent, little-boy look?"

He grinned. "You're talking wild ass females, of course."

"Well, if you insist on getting into personalities. . . ." She grinned back at him. She'd been ill at ease when he'd caught her torturing her violin. But then why should she be surprised at her complete about-face in moods? She already knew Rule had an easy way with people.

"How about that ice pack?" he pressed.

She lifted a casual shoulder. "You're the wild-ass doctor."

"Nice talk."

A giggle bubbled in her throat as she looked around, for the first time realizing that Rule was alone. "Say, where's Dana?"

"With your father-in-law. He seemed surprised that I wanted to see you. Didn't you tell him about our deal?"

"No!" Mandy clutched Rule's hand in an unconscious, pleading gesture. "He can know I'm helping you, but he mustn't know why. I don't want to raise his hopes and then fail. That would be too cruel."

Rule's eyes dropped to her half-opened lips, recalling how sweet they had tasted, how soft, yet how reluctant they had been when he first touched them. How they had become more eager, more pliant with need. Mandy was a most tempting woman.

"I won't say anything to Josh, Mandy," he promised.

When he squeezed her fingers to reassure her, she was aghast to realize she was holding his hand. With a bashful smile, she pulled from his grasp. "Thank you, Rule." She picked up her violin case and headed up the path, then turned back. Tilting her head, she studied him for a moment before an impish grin lit her face.

Rule squelched an urge to take her in his arms. "What?" he asked, smiling back.

"You look awfully fetching, holding that basket of flowers."

He moved up beside her and put a hand on the small of her back, prodding her forward. "You sure you didn't hit your head when you fell? That's crazy talk."

She laughed. What a pleasant morning it was turning out to be.

4

MANDY WAS LYING across her bed on her stomach. She'd pulled off her jeans and had an ice pack nestled against her hip. For thirty minutes, she'd been jotting down notes in a small spiral notebook. Tracing the eraser along her jaw, she frowned in thought. "I tell you, Rule, I'm at a loss. 'A square within a circle' is just too vague. But I've thought of a lot of spots we ought to check."

"Just a minute, I can't hear you," Rule called through the door. "I'll come in."

"No you don't!" she shouted, jumping up and covering herself with a corner of the patchwork quilt. "You stay in that kitchen."

She heard him laugh and relaxed, sinking back down. "How's lunch coming?"

"Dana and I are doing fine, except we can't find the jalapeño peppers."

"The what?"

"Jalapeño peppers. I can't make jalapeño omelets without jalapeño peppers."

Mandy sighed and sat up. "Barren Heath Isle is two miles off the coast of Maine, Rule. Jalapeño peppers are not considered a staple here."

"Okay then, where are your green chillies?" he called back, undaunted.

Mandy grinned in spite of herself. "Oh, for heaven's sake." She closed her notebook. "Just a minute. I'll come see if I can salvage lunch."

"What about your hip?"

"It's frozen solid. Should keep for months." She squirmed into her jeans and tucked in her blouse.

Grabbing the ice pack, she hurried into the kitchen. It was a homey place where you could almost smell the sunshine that streamed in the windows. Dana was bathed in golden sunlight where she sat cross-legged on the scarred, wooden counter. She was stirring something, completely engrossed in her work. Her tongue was poised at the corner of her mouth, and shiny black curls tumbled around her small shoulders. Mandy's heart stumbled over itself at the sight.

Rule turned to grin at her. There was flour on his nose, and he was wearing a dish towel for a makeshift apron. "You look like an escapee from a Norman Rockwell painting," she teased.

The humor in her voice made him laugh. "I'm sure you mean that as a compliment."

"Well, as long as you're sure. . . ." A smile teased her lips as she brushed past him, heading toward Dana.

"What are you making?" she inquired, breaking through the child's concentration.

Dana looked up and smiled shyly. "Instant pudding. I'm fixing dessert."

"I hope it's my favorite. Chocolate."

Dana giggled. "You know it's chocolate. It's chocolate colored."

Rule laughed. "She's not only a gourmet cook, she has a smart mouth."

Mandy turned to face him. Somehow those magnetic twinkling eyes unsettled her. "I wonder where she gets it from?" she asked, tossing the ice pack in the sink.

"Television?" he suggested innocently.

"More like a smart-aleck horse farmer from New Mexico." Drawing a clean dish towel from a drawer, she added, "Who, I might add, is a mess."

"Horse farmer," he protested as she brushed away the flour. "You make it sound like we grow them on stalks."

"You know what I mean." She took one last swipe at his nose. "How did you get flour all over your face making omelets?"

He flashed a grin. "It wasn't easy."

"Biscuits are in the oven." Dana screwed up her face. "Daddy makes real bad biscuits."

"Been making them all my life, much to my family's dismay." His eyes smiled at her as he repeated her little speech from earlier that morning almost word for word. "It relaxes me. Cats hide in the attic, but—"

"Let me guess," she interrupted. "Could it be that dogs love them?"

His beautiful, teasing smile sent a quiver up Mandy's spine.

"What cats, Daddy?" Dana asked, puzzled.

The deep sound of Rule's laughter filled the room. "Never mind, sugar."

Mandy turned away to hide a smile. "I see you've trashed my kitchen. Where's Papa Josh? Buried under the debris?"

"You're pretty sassy for a woman who's been packed in ice."

"Am I to assume from the evasive answer that Papa Josh has perished?"

"Josh is out of harm's way, asleep on the swing." He put a friendly arm across her shoulder. "Now come over here and tell me how we're going to save this omelet."

His arm about her felt warm and inviting. Without thinking, she moved a fraction closer.

Rule glanced down at her, mildly surprised. She was surveying the skilletful of eggs, unaware of his gaze. His smile softened. He'd sensed her movement more than felt it and was surprised at how her unconscious softening affected him. It was far more sensuous than any blatant come-on Savina could devise. *Down boy*, he cautioned himself. Mandy's offer hadn't been the same as Savina's.

Mandy lifted an edge of the sputtering concoction with a spatula. "The first rule of the kitchen is to make sure you have all the ingredients before leaping into the cooking phase."

Rule glanced over his shoulder at his daughter. "Now she tells us."

Dana giggled. "Daddy, you're funny."

"What about mushrooms or green peppers?" Mandy suggested.

"Yuck," Dana grunted.

"Okay, smarty-britches. If you're going to be so critical, what do you suggest we put in the omelet?"

She lifted her mixing spoon and let a thick glob drop back in the bowl. "Chocolate pudding!"

Mandy and Rule exchanged amused glances before he scooped his daughter off the counter. "Just for that, you may be excused to wash up for lunch." He took the pudding bowl and stuck it in the refrigerator. "Take notice of those elbows and those ears, too. You look like you've been rooting with pigs."

Dana burst out in a fit of giggles and ran from the room making very convincing oinking sounds.

Rule shook his head. "There's a reform school in that kid's future."

Mandy laughed. "She's very outgoing."

Rule glanced over at the door where Dana had disappeared. "She's fine with me, but she gets pretty miserable if I get too far away." He was speaking in a low, confidential voice. "She's afraid I'll leave her and never come back."

"Because her mother deserted her?" Mandy berated herself inwardly as soon as the words were out of her mouth.

When Rule's gaze returned to her, his rich, dark eyes had frosted over. "Being deserted by someone you love is no picnic, Mandy."

She could tell by the edge in his voice that he was not merely talking about Dana. Somewhere deep inside this man, there was the lingering pain of a five-year-old boy, deserted by his father. Mandy's heart went out to him. She took his hands in hers. "I'm sorry, Rule. It was a stupid question."

She saw the change in his eyes and smiled faintly. "Friends?"

Rule laced his fingers with hers and held on. His eyes roamed her face. It intrigued him to watch a slow blush pinken her cheeks, and his features gentled. "Mandy?" he murmured.

"Hmmmm?"

"How do you feel about bologna sandwiches?"

"Why?"

"Because our lunch is burning."

AN HOUR LATER, they were hiking across a field, hard at the hunt. Dana had run ahead, chasing butterflies and picking wildflowers.

Mandy referred to her notebook. "There's a tree near the wood's edge. It's got a big knothole in it." She shrugged. "I don't know, Rule. The clue's so vague. I just thought we'd better check anything resembling a circle."

He smiled at her. "You're the boss."

She felt a pleasant flutter in her stomach and turned away, gesturing. "Over there, toward the stand of pines."

Seconds later they heard a loud rustling and decided to investigate. Behind a clump of brush they were surprised to see Henry Poppy, squatting in the grass, digging with a salad fork.

"Uncle Henry?" Rule called quietly.

At the sound of his name, Henry popped up and wobbled around to face them. "My boy," he protested. "You're protruding!"

At the mention of the word *protruding*, Mandy's glance strayed to Rule's denim-clad hips. It was a visual trip her brain had not authorized, but the excursion was proving to be pleasant, nonetheless. *Protruding* wasn't the word she'd have chosen to describe what there was to see, but Rule's jeans certainly did fit him well, contouring his anatomy in a singularly masculine way.

"Do you agree, Mandy?"

She whipped her gaze up to meet his, hoping he hadn't caught her staring. His eyes were twinkling devilishly. He had. Her cheeks smoldered. "Er—I'm sorry. What were you saying?"

"Something about protruding," he reminded her with a grin.

"Tut, tut." Henry waved a chubby hand. "The young lady's protrusion is quite welcome." He beamed at Mandy.

"A flash of sanity," Rule mused aloud, adding fire to her cheeks.

"What, my boy?"

"Nothing, Uncle Henry. We were just passing by." He put a hand at Mandy's back and walked forward. "What are you doing?"

Henry gestured with his fork, indicating four rocks that would have made the general shape of a square if you were playing connect the rocks. "Isn't it obtuse, young man?"

Rule nodded. "I'd say so."

"A square, my boy. In a circle." Henry then pointed to a scrub oak nearby. Its shadow took in the rocks and appeared nearly round at this time of the day.

"I see." Rule cast Mandy a furtive look as Henry dropped to his knees again.

Mandy's eyes widened. She was hesitant to disturb a man who was clearly disturbed enough. "Uh... Henry?"

He stopped gouging the dirt with his fork and lumbered back up. "What is it now?" he puffed, frowning.

"Where's Maybelle?"

"Why, naturally, she's scuba diving."

"Naturally." Mandy shrugged helplessly. "I feel so silly—Eeeek!" she squealed when chubby, tweed arms grabbed and squeezed her around the middle.

"Not at all, my dear. You feel quite squishy to me." He backed away, grinning, delighted with himself for his brilliant discovery. "Now that that's settled, I really must get back to my work. Ta ta."

He hunched down, his back to them as he returned to stabbing the rocky soil.

Smothering his mirth, Rule took Mandy's arm, guiding her away. When they were out of earshot, she whispered, "Your uncle keeps grabbing me."

"I noticed," he said chuckling. "I'm beginning to have my doubts about his insanity."

She couldn't help but laugh. "What do you suppose he'll do when the shadow starts moving?"

"Probably trench the island."

Mandy shook her head in amazement. "I wonder if he ever returns to reality?"

"As a tourist, maybe."

She was suddenly curious about something. "Why do you suppose Maybelle is scuba diving?"

Rule's smile grew lopsided. "Insanity doesn't just run in my family. It gallops."

"Your dad wasn't crazy, though. I understand he was a genius inventor."

Rule turned away, the muscles in his jaw flexing. "I suppose."

Noting his change of mood, Mandy touched his hand. "I'm sorry, Rule. If you'd rather not talk about him. . . ."

He shrugged disinterestedly. "All I know about my father is what my mother told me. He invented a piece of equipment that revolutionized the industrial weaving loom and made millions. At some big banquet in his honor, my father met Lydia Ravencroft. Not long after that, he ran off with her. End of story."

Subdued, Mandy asked, "Where's your mother now?"

Rule squinted up at the sky. "She died when I was sixteen. I've been on my own ever since."

"Oh," she murmured, unable to think of anything comforting or helpful to say.

They reached a gully, and Rule helped her across. His fingers were strong, yet gentle. When she stepped to the other side, they were very close. Mandy smiled into his eyes. "Your mother would be proud if she could see what sort of man you turned out to be—trying to save the horses and all."

The soft compliment caught him off guard and his expression softened. "Thanks."

"It's the truth."

Her scent reached up to him, sending a rush through his brain. He had an urgent desire to sample again that hot, honeyed taste of her mouth.

A breeze ruffled the loose wisps of hair about her face and he wanted badly to touch them, to pull her into his arms and make love to her here on the grass. He'd been with enough women to know that Mandy would be a fiery lover, and his insides burned to taste her fully. Yet he didn't dare touch her. It wasn't just because his daughter was nearby. He knew that if he took Mandy by surprise as he had last night, she would stiffen and retreat from him again.

He had to keep reminding himself that she was with him to help her father-in-law, not to ease his lust.

Reluctantly, he drew his hand away from her arm and put it in his pocket, muttering, "Hadn't we better move on?"

His tone seemed strained, but his eyes told her nothing of what he might be thinking. Feeling awkward, she stepped away, indicating the direction with a nod. "The tree's over there."

Dana scampered by, waving her bouquet. "Daddy, I'm gona make a new flower crown for ZeZe. All red flowers."

"Good, sweetheart. We'll be close by."

The little girl plopped down and began to weave the ruby petals together.

"She loves that toy," Mandy observed.

"Yes. Her comfort object, the pediatrician calls it." He smiled wanly. "The thing should be burned. She drags it with her everywhere." He looked lovingly at his daughter. "The health department has probably already sent around memos about it."

He was smiling again. Whatever had been wrong seemed to be forgotten. She touched his arm. "Here's the tree . . . the big pecan there."

When Mandy pointed out the large hole, she grimaced. "I didn't remember it being that high. Maybe if you lift me I can reach it."

His gaze became appraising as he looked her up and down. "How's your balance?"

"Oh, poo, you're making this sound harder than it is," she scolded as she lifted her hands to his shoulders. "Boost me up."

After a slight hesitation, he shrugged in acquiescence. Lacing his fingers together, he made a stirrup for her foot. "Up you go."

When she stepped into his hands, he catapulted her up until her knees were level with his shoulders. She sucked in a frightened cry, grabbing the tree trunk to keep from toppling backward. Unknowingly she pressed her thigh into his face.

A muffled sound came from Rule's throat. Mandy lurched away, embarrassed, causing him to lose his hold on her foot. With lightning reflexes, he grabbed her hips, keeping her from falling, but Mandy flailed out blindly. Her arms curled around his head, crushing her breasts against his mouth.

"I don't think this is working," she squeaked, clutching for dear life.

"Why would you think that?" he muttered into her breasts, sounding edgy.

She could feel the roughness of his jaw through her blouse, and his breath was moist against her breasts. She wriggled in his arms, shifting her hands to press down on his shoulders. "Raise me up. I can stand on your shoulders."

"Try not to fall backward this time."

"I won't," she cried morosely, embarrassed to her core. "Just do it!"

With a grunt and a powerful thrust, Rule lifted her high enough so that she could get her sneakers balanced on his shoulders. He grabbed her ankles to steady her as she got a firm hold on the tree.

She bent to look into the hole. While scanning the darkness inside, she wondered grudgingly if he could have boosted her all the way in the first place.

"Are you okay?" He sounded hoarse.

"I guess. What about you? Did you strain anything?"

He muttered something she couldn't hear.

"What?"

"I'll survive," he grumbled. "Just look in the hole."

"Okay, okay." She rummaged around. "Nothing but acorns . . . and a deserted nest."

"No fifty-million-dollar bills?" he asked, feeling uncharacteristically irritable. That scent of hers clung to every inch of her, and it was tormenting him. He had a foolish urge to nuzzle the calf that kept brushing against his hair.

"Oh, did I forget to mention the bills?" She picked up a handful of acorns and dropped them on his head in peevish glee. "That should teach you to manhandle me."

"Ouch. Is that the thanks I get for saving your bacon?" He squelched his mounting desires, moving slightly to relieve the painful pressure their unintentional intimate contact had produced in his jeans. His actions elicited a squeal from her.

"Don't move!" she cried, snagging the tree again. "Rule Danforth, you have an ugly streak of sadism in you."

"*I* have an ugly streak of sadism, she says." His mumbled response was ripe with dark overtones.

"What is that supposed to mean?"

"Forget it," he gritted out the words. "Are you ready to come down?"

She scowled at him. "Do you think you could use more finesse this time?"

He reached up and grasped her hips. "I can try."

He lowered her slowly. Every centimeter of her hips, stomach and breasts was forced to rub against him. It seemed like an eternity before her feet touched the earth. Stepping away from him, she smoothed her shirt into place, avoiding his eyes. She felt feverish and light-headed, as if she might be coming down with the flu.

"Was that better?" he asked, his tone grim.

Mandy shot him a suspicious look. It couldn't simply have been her imagination. It had to have been with malice aforethought that he had slid her across him so that she was made well aware of his manhood! Unfortunately, she had no proof. There was the remote possibility that he had merely lowered her very carefully.

Prudently swallowing her accusations, she remarked dryly, "I'm impressed. If all else fails, you can always get a job as a forklift." She fumbled in her breast pocket for her list. Her fingers felt like cooked noodles and her legs weren't faring much better. Why did his touch have such a debilitating effect on her?

She scanned the list, wanting nothing more than to get away. "Next is a deserted root cellar. Are you coming?" Without waiting for his answer, she spun around and headed toward the field where Dana sat, adorning her stuffed zebra with crimson poppies.

Rule leaned against the tree, feeling weary. Coming in contact with Mandy McRae was a crippling experience. He exhaled slowly, watching the sway of her hips as she pranced off. It was painful.

5

FOUR DAYS and four nonsensical phrases later, Rule and Mandy were no closer to finding the treasure than they had been that first morning. Neither were the other relatives. Maybelle had had some luck on her dive in the cove. She'd dredged up three cracked china plates, a tire and a mannequin. The muck-covered dummy had almost given her apoplexy when she'd thought she'd found a body. That was the extent of the booty to date.

After the ordeal at the tree, both Mandy and Rule had kept a respectable distance, each for his or her own reasons, and their partnership was flourishing.

They had been all over the island looking in every conceivable nook and cranny. They had not found what they had been looking for, but they found something that they hadn't expected. A budding kinship. They learned that they both enjoyed long walks, stormy nights and steaks grilled medium rare.

Mandy looked forward to spending her time with Rule and Dana. She enjoyed the pleasant evening hours they passed, rocking on Josh's porch swing, laughing, teasing and finally just sitting quietly with Dana asleep on her lap.

This morning Mandy was finishing some mending, waiting for Rule to come with the fifth clue. As she repaired a seam on one of Josh's shirts, Rule's image came to her: those thick curls that lay in attractive disarray across his brow, that wide mouth, vivid eyes that were sometimes ripe with humor, other times dark and un-fathomable.

She shifted in her chair and jabbed at the fabric. Fortunately, she had been able to put Rule's kiss entirely from her thoughts. Well, almost entirely, she amended, heeding a nagging little voice.

What had happened between them in the bride's garden was an unfortunate misunderstanding, something she hardly ever dwelled on. It was true that she'd been unable to sleep well lately. But she hadn't spent all that much time staring up at the ceiling recalling his lips or the sheltering hardness of his arms. . . .

The familiar thud of Rule's boots mounting the porch jarred Mandy from her wayward thoughts, and she pricked her finger.

The screen door creaked open and Dana rushed in. "Hi, Miss Mandy!" She rushed into the young woman's arms for a hug.

"Mmmmm." Mandy gathered her up, kissing her cheek. "Are we ready to hunt for treasure today?"

Dana shook her curls, beaming. "Mr. Josh is going to tell me a story about a dragon. Then, ZeZe and me'll fix you and Josh and Daddy lunch."

The door swung shut as Rule entered. "That means we'll be having raisin bread, milk and Oreo cookies." He strode to where Mandy was holding his daughter. "Come, Dana, we don't want to bother Miss Mandy all the time, do we?"

Mandy glanced up, curious. "She's no bother, Rule."

He lifted Dana into his arms. "Josh is going to work in his garden out back. Since it's hard for him to bend, he wants you to help him plant the seeds."

"Oh, goodie," Dana squeaked. "I like gardens." She screwed up her face as though she had second thoughts.

"But I won't plant spinach. Tell him that, Daddy. No spinach!"

Rule threw back his head and laughed. "I'll tell him no such thing, young lady." He tossed her across his shoulder like a sack of feed. "You plant what he wants planted, or no dragon stories."

Dana made hoarse, huffing sounds with each step Rule took, and Mandy fretted that she might be hurt. Just before they disappeared outside, Dana lifted her head and waved gaily.

Grinning at the little girl's antics, Mandy stood and straightened her gray cotton sweater and slacks before she picked up the mending.

When the sewing things had been put away, Rule returned. "'A doughnut's fate,'" he recited, running a distracted hand through his hair. His smile was gone, and Mandy wondered at his mood.

"The clue?" she asked.

"What did Lydia do, eat her fortune?" His expression was sober, and he seemed to have something on his mind besides the hunt.

She watched him in uneasy anticipation. "Is something wrong, Rule?"

He held her gaze with serious eyes, then exhaled slowly as though he were about to say something that was very hard. "Why didn't you tell me about Rebecca?" The question had come out simply, but each word had dropped like a burning coal on Mandy's heart.

"Why...how did you..."

"Emma said something about how much Dana looked like Rebecca. I asked her who Rebecca was." His voice was flat. "Why didn't you tell me you had a daughter who had died?"

Mandy's insides constricted painfully at the word. She drew her eyes away, saying simply, "It's my own personal pain, Rule."

"Mandy, look at me."

Startled at the distress in his tone, she obeyed. When she met his gaze again, his eyes were bleak, but his lips were twisted in a sardonic smile. "For a while I let myself believe all you wanted to do was help Josh. That your motives were just what they appeared to be."

Before she could defend herself, he went on. "I had no idea you just wanted us around so that you could use my daughter as a substitute for Rebecca."

Mandy felt as if she'd been slammed in the stomach with a wrecking ball. "That's a cruel thing to suggest," she murmured in confusion.

"It's also a cruel thing to do," he returned, his expression unyielding.

Her shock had dissipated enough to allow righteous anger to rampage up her spine. She blurted hotly, "You have a *nasty* way of jumping to conclusions, Mr. Danforth. What's wrong with showing a little kindness?"

"A *little* kindness?" He laughed bitterly. "You rock her to sleep on your lap. You call her 'honey' and 'darling'. You kiss and hug her every time she comes within arm's length. Damn it, woman, she talks about you constantly."

Mandy was quivering with fury. "You still have no right to make ridiculous accusations!"

"Ridiculous?" His nostrils flared. "Who's kidding who? Dana's mother walked out on her when she was three. Dana hasn't gotten over it." Savage pain flashed in his eyes as he muttered, "I don't intend to let her go through being deserted a second time. Try to think about my daughter's needs, not just your own."

"That's unfair," Mandy cried. "You're just insecure because your father walked out on you. You have no right to condemn my actions just because of what happened to you."

He looked as if he'd been slapped, and slapped hard. She bit her lip, feeling disgusted with herself for her unthinking remark. "I—I shouldn't have said that," she admitted, but still determined that she was right, she added, "Surely you can't object to my showing Dana a little kindness."

"Are you sure a six-year-old can tell the difference between mere kindness and love?"

His rough whisper stunned Mandy. Yet, even in her distress, she knew that Rule was saying what he thought was necessary to protect his little girl from more heartache.

Having Dana around had been so comforting these past few days. Was there any truth to what Rule was saying? Was there the slightest possibility that she was using the little girl to satisfy her own need to have her daughter back? She hoped not. The last thing in the world she wanted to do was to hurt Dana. She swallowed several times to try to dislodge the hard lump that had formed in her throat. She could think of nothing to say to aid in her defense.

Fighting tears, she avoided his eyes and turned away, toward the door. "I—I'll remember," she promised through trembling lips. "Maybe we'd better go."

TWO DAYS dragged by. Mandy and Rule passed them in a tense truce, with Mandy being careful to treat Dana with the cordiality of a guest. It was hard not to take the child onto her lap or pull her into her arms to accept a wet, sticky kiss, but Mandy was determined to abide by Rule's wishes. After all, Dana was his child.

It was Sunday, the seventh day of the fortune hunt. Rule arrived alone, saying that Dana was already with Josh, busy at work in the garden.

"The clue is, 'lost and green'." He shook his head. "Clear as mud."

He seemed more at ease today. That lightened Mandy's spirits considerably. Apparently her forebearance where Dana was concerned was paying off.

"Lost and green," she repeated, searching for possible meanings. After several minutes, inspiration dawned, and she grinned up at Rule. "The secret garden. Why haven't I thought of that before? Rumor has it that Lydia seduced her lovers there—before she married your father, of course. Maybe she left her treasure there, too."

Rule expressed mild surprise, then grinned. "Sounds like she left treasure there several times."

She eyed him narrowly. "A totally male reaction."

"I'm gratified you think so."

She responded in a shockingly physical way to the intense glint in his eye. Like warm oil, the feeling seeped from the center of her body outward, making her nipples grow taut. Turning away, she grabbed up a shawl, intent on hiding the embarrassing evidence. "It's a little cool this morning for this sundress," she explained weakly.

To her surprise, Rule took the crocheted garment from her and slipped it across her shoulders, murmuring, "Seems warm to me." His fingers lingered against her skin, causing a tiny quiver along her spine.

Without quite looking at him, she said, "Let's go see Lydia's trysting place."

Though she hurried to the door, Rule's long strides got him there first. He pushed open the screen. His smile had a raging sexuality about it, difficult to ignore. As she brushed passed him, Mandy began to have doubts that a trysting place was a smart place to go with a man like Rule Danforth.

"The garden's pretty deep in the woods beyond the meadow, Rule." Mandy pointed, indicating the direction.

"Near the tree with the hole full of painful acorns?"

He was grinning at her, reminding her of their fiasco that first day. She fought a smile. "Generally."

"Say!" a voice called from some distance away. "Mind if we join you?"

Mandy and Rule turned to see Steppy jogging toward them along the path that led from the mansion to the cottage. He was holding his camera to steady it, though it hung from a strap around his neck. Savina was tottering along behind as best she could in her five-inch heels. "Wait, Steppy, hon," she called. "I can't run in these shoes."

"I told you to change them, Savi," he called back. "How do you expect to do any good hobbled that way?"

She giggled and grasped his elbow for support. "You like my legs in high heels." She looked up and saw Rule with Mandy and her smile faded. "Oh, *damn*," she muttered under her breath, then clamped her jaws together and looked away.

Mandy noticed, and wondered about it. Savina had never been very friendly, but this was rude, even for her. She cast a glance at Rule. His expression was pleasant enough. It couldn't be anything he'd done. Stumped, she turned back. "Hello, Savina, Steppy. How is everything?"

"Fine. Just wondered where you two were going." Practically before the words were uttered, he dropped to his knees, surprising everyone, especially Savina, who'd been clinging to his arm.

"Steppy, you almost made me fall. What are you doing down there?"

"Just a sec, hon. Perfect shot of a ladybug." The shutter snapped and he stood, grinning. "Love ladybugs. Well, as I was saying, where are you two heading?"

"Treasure hunting, Steppy," Rule said. "That's pretty much the reason we're here."

Steppy laughed. "Oh, sure. I know that. I just figured we might tag along."

"I'd rather not, Steppy," Savina pouted prettily. "We don't need them. Come on." She tugged at the collar of his knit shirt, then whispered something in his ear.

He chuckled wickedly and slung his arm around her neck. "Never mind, people. Savina's right. It's every man for himself this trip." They sauntered off, entwined, without a backward glance.

Mandy stared after them. "Savina said she was going to get in on the treasure somehow. Do you suppose that chuckle means she's found a way?" She looked back at Rule.

He was grinning down at her. "Do everblooming violas bloom all summer?"

Her lips twitched in a smile. "Damned if you know," she reminded him.

His smile faded slightly and it struck Mandy that he'd recalled when they'd had this conversation before. It had been just after what Mandy now thought of as The Kiss. Feeling oddly shy, she turned back to scrutinize the disappearing couple. "Do you think Savina can compete with ladybugs?"

Rule's quick laughter sounded every bit as wicked as Steppy's had. Suspicious about the undertone in his laughter, Mandy asked, "What do you mean by that?"

Placing his hand in the small of her back to coax her forward, he said, "Not a thing."

Mandy was a firm believer in gut reactions. She was having a strong one now. She would not be put off. "Savina approached you first, didn't she?" Irritation tingled along her spine at the very idea! Her ire was irrational and misplaced, she knew. She and Rule had a business deal. Nothing personal. But knowing that didn't seem to help. "What did she do, offer you her . . . sex?" she asked a bit brittlely.

His eyes glittered with amusement. "Where have you been keeping your mind?"

"I got the idea from you, buster." She elbowed him. "Remember?"

"Ouch!" He grabbed her arm, chuckling. "Yes. I recall it vividly. A night that will live in infamy—"

"Savina did, didn't she?" When Rule didn't answer, she groaned, writhing inside. "*You kissed her! You actually kissed her, too!*"

"Let's just say I was there."

"Well. . . .?" Mandy's voice was a whisper of high anxiety. "What happened? How did you happen to turn down such a tasty offer?"

"Does it matter?"

"But . . . but you're with me, and I didn't offer you—"

"I remember exactly what you didn't offer me." There was faint amusement in his voice, and something else. Something just beneath the humor that disturbed her, yet made her blood race.

"Can we forget about Savina?" he asked after a moment.

"With pleasure," she snapped, pivoting away and stalking toward the meadow.

"Mandy?" He caught up with her. "Let's just say I'm not sorry I turned her down, and let it go at that. Okay?"

That funny little prickle of irritation disintegrated, and Mandy felt more at ease. Looking into his earnest eyes, she had no choice but to nod her agreement. "Okay," she whispered, meaning it.

Ten minutes later, they entered the woods. The ground was a tangle of vines and leaves, and the air was chilly. It had the nutty, damp smell of fertile earth and decaying leaves. Mandy inhaled deeply, enjoying the heavy scent. "Over that way, I think." She pointed deeper into the shadows.

It was dark and sunless; the going was tough. Mandy finally took Rule's arm and hung on in order to keep from tripping in her flimsy sandals. The hem of her sundress kept snagging on things, slowing them down. This was one time she thought Maybelle's safari attire made a lot of sense.

They clambered over a fallen branch. When something furry scurried by Mandy's leg, she squealed and leaped at Rule, who took her one hundred and twenty pounds squarely in the chest with a "Wooooof."

She grabbed his neck. "Did you see that?"

"See what?" He sounded winded as he encircled her waist with his arms to help support her.

"That wolf!"

She could feel his chuckle. "Are you sure it wasn't a panic-stricken squirrel?"

She blinked and looked up to meet his eyes. "Do you think so?"

He nodded, his eyes sparkling with laughter. "Unless Lydia and Arnold imported wolves to the island."

She felt stupid and looked away, mumbling, "I suppose you think I'm an awful coward."

"It never crossed my mind." He inclined his head fractionally closer. The look he gave her was purposeful, the look of a man who was about to kiss a woman. She stared, her eyes wide. "Er—Rule..." Untensing her arms, she let them slide down to rest on his chest. "I...think we're close."

"We're way past close," he corrected softly.

"I mean, the garden." Her legs felt like lead weights as she scrambled unsteadily away. "Follow me," she breathed unevenly. Grabbing Rule like that had been stupid. Very stupid! Paying little attention to where she was going, she thrashed through some shrubbery, instantly stunned into paralysis by a bewitching sanctuary.

Her nostrils filled with sweet, nectared purity. Dainty pink flowers peeked out from amid a silver-leafed carpet of ground cover. Climbing scarlet roses and large-leafed ferns had gone berserk, left to their own fertile devices. The rose vines had woven themselves into sheltering walls of intoxicating beauty that climbed toward heaven. There was but one oval window of sunlight above their heads. Yellow columbines turned their trumpetlike petals upward to drink the sunshine that flooded over them, warming and nourishing the hidden trysting place.

"Fantastic," Rule remarked quietly. "I would never have guessed a place like this existed."

"That's what I'm here for," Mandy said, her voice high pitched in agitation.

"Thanks for the reminder. I forgot for a minute."

She cleared her throat, ignoring the husky implication of his words. "Yes, well... According to the rumors—" Mandy eased down on the warm ground and pulled off a sandal, dumping a pebble out and rubbing the sore spot it had made on her heel "—Lydia supposedly seduced her lovers with some sort of sensuous dance..."

Rule joined her on the ground, his eyes drinking her in. "Couldn't have been as sensuous as the way you take off a sandal."

She looked up, startled. "What?"

"I said, would you mind if I kissed you?"

Her lips opened in astonishment. "That's not what you said."

"It's what I was thinking. Would you mind?"

"You... you already have."

"Again." He dipped his face closer.

She swallowed. She hadn't been able to get over that first kiss in the bride's garden. At long last she was admitting it, but this was rotten timing. She should have faced it sooner, that way she could have thought out some means of dealing with what was happening now. She hedged. "Rule...we made a deal. A business deal."

He was very close and moving closer, a stirring, electric presence, pulling her to him. As he took her in his arms, she watched without the power to resist or speak.

"Mandy, I know you didn't offer yourself to me in our partnership, but that doesn't keep me from wanting you." His breath was like a pleasant breeze against her cheek. "I've been obsessed with the desire to make love to you ever since that first kiss...." He covered her mouth with his; his breath was heated, his tongue compelling.

Her mind reeled with the feeling of his body against hers. Fearful, she wrestled her lips from his, protesting feebly, "What are you doing?"

"Losing my mind," he murmured softly, his lips teasing hers again. His alluring male scent battered away at her resolve as he pressed her down into nature's soft bed. He was lethal. His taste and smell were delicious poisons, killing all reason. Her head tipped back, and without conscious thought she accepted his kiss more fully as his searching tongue eased her lips into a desperate compliance.

Her brain screamed for logic. This thing that was happening between them was totally inappropriate! She didn't love this stranger. She didn't want to. Peter had been her one true love. She had no intention of tarnishing his memory by becoming a cheap plaything for the first pair of tight jeans that sauntered by. So why, then, was she here, on her back, resisting nothing, anticipating everything?

As his kisses trailed along her jaw, her body began to ache with a fascinating pain. She could feel her chasteness slipping further and further away with every nip of his questing lips.

"Rule, this is insane," she gasped against his cheek.

"I know. Danforth curse..." He dipped his tongue in her ear.

She sucked in her breath, arching against him. If she had to give a name to the choking need that was engulfing her, it would have to be lust. Pure, unadulterated lust. She'd never felt such helpless desire for a man in her life, not even with Peter, the man she'd loved, respected, married and borne a child by. She'd always been contented with him, but never had she felt this raging insanity of mind and body—the urge to take a man and consume him whole. This lathered compulsion was unhealthy. It had to be. No one could live very long caught up in such physical overindulgence!

When his lips lifted to sear along her neck, she pleaded, on the verge of tears, "Love me..." It startled her. She'd meant to say something else entirely, something like "Let me go!" But instead all she could say—whimper—cry—were those two words, over and over, as her fingers, shaky and weak, fumbled scandalously with the buttons of his shirt.

"Mandy...Mandy..." His low, urgent sigh scattered the last vestiges of her determination to resist. She felt him quiver as her cold fingers spread the fabric, sliding it off his muscled shoulders. His reaction gave her a feeling of heady power, and her hands moved down on their own. Madness had crept into her deepest being, for what she was doing was truly deranged, without basis in logic or good sense. She was actually undressing this man.

Why? her brain shrieked. But the desperate question fell on deaf ears. His belt slid away, then his jeans and underwear. She knew a suffocating breathlessness when she saw him aroused, pulsating, ready. For her. Urgency spread a prickling fire from her core out through her quivering limbs. She, too, was pulsating. Theirs had become a primeval concert that nothing could prevent being played out to the final, crashing crescendo.

Rule's eyes glowed down at her, full of lusty promise—a powerful aphrodisiac. She held and savored the richness of his look as his fingers moved gently to relieve her from the bondage of her clothes.

Once free, she was overwhelmed by lush sensations as his long thighs, lean and muscular, slid intimately over hers. His mouth was touching hers again, nibbling, his tongue flicking her teeth, his hands melting every fiber of her being. She was burning out of control. The soft mat of his chest against her naked breasts made her feel deliriously giddy. She curled her arms around him, allowing her head to loll back in the cushion of leaves.

Their breathing had become love labored and heavy in the woodland quiet. He pressed his lips against the pulse at her throat, then moved down to nuzzle and gladden the taut tips of her breasts. She half sighed, half moaned as his hands traveled along the curve of her waist, down to cup a hip. Hot, demanding lips followed. She gasped with the thrill of delights she knew were soon to be enjoyed as his lips meandered down to taste, at last, forbidden fruit. She sucked in a shaky breath, closing her eyes, enslaved in a prison of pure sensation.

Her mind shrank back, helpless to intercede, at a loss to interpret what was happening to the sensible, clear-thinking woman she had always been. Rule was leading her where rational thought had no place, where one flings away the mask of civilization to become one with man's most primitive emotions.

Mandy encircled him with her legs, shuddering in awe at the enflamed explosions he was inspiring within her. He had carried her to the gates of paradise—and beyond. She laughed and cried, feeling lost, yet flying free amid pagan wonders.

A fine film of moisture cooled her skin, and she shivered with equal shares of release and a new, growing need for his encompassing warmth. "Darling," she whispered, her voice quavering with want. "Come to me."

Kissing her just below the naval, he murmured, "One second . . ." Turning away slightly he pulled something from his jeans pocket. Mandy couldn't quite see what he was doing, but she could hear a rustling. "You're not leaving?" she breathed, her body aching for him.

His chuckle was deep. "Not likely—just taking care of business."

She blinked, surprised and a bit disconcerted when she realized he was slipping on protection. Out here, in the middle of nowhere?

He moved up to blanket her with the angular strength of his body. His face was tender, almost boyish as he smiled, "Mandy, love..." His voice broke with the depth of his emotion.

The glimpse of his tender vulnerability filled her heart, and she forgot her momentary disquiet. Pulling his face to hers, she kissed him wantonly, a stranger to herself in his arms. She wanted more, wanted to give more, than she ever had in her life. With heedless abandon, she opened herself to him, moaning her joy as he entered her. He began to move slowly, exquisitely slowly, as if he intended to spend the rest of his life within her tight, intimate embrace.

She looked into his eyes. They were dear, reassuring. She smiled up at him, a tremulous, faulty smile with lips numbed by pleasure.

His thrusts became more urgent as he plunged deeper and deeper. Mandy's lips were parted, her eyes squeezed shut as her whole being centered on each powerful lunge that brought with it a white-hot spear of delight that lifted her up—up, until she was once again spiraling, dizzy and disoriented in the mystic world of ultimate release.

Even as her body's quaking subsided, draining of all tension, and glowing under Rule's expertise, she wept, hating herself for her weakness. "Oh Peter..." she whimpered in anguish, tears sliding from the corners of her eyes. How could she have done this to him? How could she have relished this stranger's body so totally and forgotten her promise to Peter?

So lost was Mandy in her anguish that she did not fully realize how still Rule had gone above her. It was only when the protective warmth of his body lifted away, and the moistness they had shared began to cool her skin, that she opened her eyes to look up at him. Shock filled her brain at his expression.

If the sparks in his eyes could have leapt out at her, she would have been ablaze. "Cover yourself," he growled, tossing her her shawl.

Feebly she obeyed, feeling muddled. Before she had grasped the full reality of his anger, he had turned away and was dragging on his clothes.

"What is it?" she asked, her voice hoarse, nearly inaudible. She reached out and touched his naked shoulder.

He drew away and jerked his shirt up to cover the taut flesh. With a muttered curse, he vaulted up to tower over her.

"What's the matter?" he gritted, obviously working for control. "Not a thing." Though anger raged on in his brown eyes, his face was now frighteningly passive. "Except my name doesn't happen to be Peter."

6

HE PIVOTED on his heel and stalked out of the garden, leaving her to stare after him, horrified. Peter? Mandy pondered, her mind still clouded by their recently spent passion. Where had Rule learned his name? She shivered, pulling the shawl more securely about her. With leaden arms, she reached for her dress and was astonished by how heavy the thin fabric felt. Struggling into her clothes was a gargantuan effort. She had no strength left in her quivering limbs. Rule's potent lovemaking had drained her completely—raked from her every last scrap of pent-up desire and need, not to mention all dignity and honor.

"Oh Lord . . ." she moaned, pulling her legs up and resting her tearstained face on her knees. "I don't believe this."

"Neither do I," muttered a very familiar voice.

Her head shot up. How had he managed to return so quietly? Rule was standing just inside the garden, his expression grim. He was so physically arresting that her heart leaped against her ribs. Raven curls lay in unkempt disarray across his tanned forehead, a silent reminder of how recently her fevered hands had scattered and caressed them. His legs were braced wide, his arms hanging tensely at his sides.

Standing there in the shadows, he seemed cast in bronze. It was only his expressive eyes that gave lie to the illusion. This was no statue. He was a man of flesh and feelings. His hooded gaze was alive with searing contempt. Yet there was something else in the brown depths, something behind the heat. Far from sinister, this strange, lurking entity gave her watery limbs the strength to stand and face his wrath.

"I—I'm glad you came back," she stammered.

His nostrils flared. For an instant Mandy feared that he would unleash a scathing insult, but he only muttered, "You'd better put on your sandals."

She watched his face. Dark emotions seemed to come and go. Through it all, his stare remained fixed on her face. She could tell he was trying to appear unmoved, but he was filled with so much fierce resentment that it was impossible to disguise it completely.

"Rule . . ." She ignored her sandals and walked over to him. "Did I actually say Peter?"

His gaze fought free of hers as he distanced himself emotionally. "Forget it," he bit out. "We'd better get back."

Hating the hurt in his eyes, she took one of his big hands in hers. The move drew his startled gaze back. "What must you think of me?" she whispered, tears welling against her will.

His face was set as his eyes searched hers.

She shook her head. "I'm sorry. I cherish Peter's memory. I—I've been alone a long time—" her voice quavered and broke. Unable to continue, she turned away and plucked up her sandals, unsteadily putting them on.

"Peter was your husband?"

He had moved up behind her. Mandy dreaded turning to face him, but she knew she must. When their eyes met, she inched her chin up gravely. "Yes. He was my husband. I loved him very much."

Rule stared at her, his scowl darkening. "You loved him so much that you fantasize about him no matter who's making love to you."

She felt the sting of the slap in her hand before she realized that she'd flung her arm toward his face, hitting him hard. "How dare you say such an ugly thing!"

He grabbed her outstretched hand, his face contorted with disgust and despair. "Mandy, I'm sorry. I didn't mean that."

She yanked her hand away. "Just what did you mean?" Her anger was a living, breathing thing writhing inside her, pulling her apart. How could he think she was the kind of woman who'd allow just any man to make love to her? Was his opinion of women that low?

He took a step toward her, gripping her by the shoulders. His touch was gentler than his expression. "I just meant you can't go on making love to a dead man forever. You have to go on living."

She bristled. Unsure why his remark pricked her so, she demanded, "And your idea of living is a hot little tumble in the woods? How sensitive of you!"

"Mandy..."

"And as far as—how did you so quaintly put it?— fantasizing about someone else no matter who you're making love to? Well, *buster*, I wasn't the one with a condom in my jeans pocket all ready for sex at a moment's notice! What do you macho cowboys do—keep a few tucked away with your beer money for rowdy Saturday nights in town?"

Her outrage made little sense. After all, Rule had been considering her welfare by opting for "safe sex", but Mandy couldn't help herself. Though the feeling was unreasonable, it hurt her to think that Rule was so totally prepared to have sex with any woman he might stumble across.

"Mandy, I've been single for over three years," Rule explained, looking stung. "Yes, I pack condoms just like I pack shaving cream. But this wasn't as random an act as you think. I gave it a lot of thought before I put the damned thing in my pocket. You touch me, Mandy, and I want to make love to you. Is that so terrible?"

She was listening, but she didn't want to hear what he was saying, didn't want to be moved by his words. When she neither responded nor reacted, just continued to glare, he went on. "And I wanted to protect you. In the real world it's only being responsible to use pro—"

"How noble of you," she scoffed. Feeling confused and upset, she struck out blindly. "Mr. Rule Responsible! And that makes everything all right?"

"It seemed very right to me," he murmured.

"Well, I'll thank you to be responsible with somebody else the next time you feel the urge." Straightening indignantly, she brushed away his arms and hurried by him. "As you said before, we'd better go." Before she'd reached the garden's edge, she realized that stalking off would accomplish nothing. They had to get this thing finished between them. She twisted around to face him again.

Rule's eyes were golden embers of frustration burning behind dark lashes. That unsettling look touched a quickness within her, and she averted her gaze. "Rule," she whispered, desperately, "please. If you're a gentleman, you'll pretend this . . . thing never happened."

There was a long, dead moment between them before Rule retorted. "Pretend? Like when you pretended I was Peter?" His tone was dark with scorn.

Her flush was a disturbing combination of remembered pleasure and alarm. She looked up, focusing on his unsmiling mouth. She dared not attempt eye-to-eye contact. "I mean, please forget it happened."

"That I can't do."

"If I explain...?" Through a tremulous sigh, she whispered, "Rule, I called out Peter's name because I—I couldn't believe any other man could make me feel so—" She ran a trembling hand across her lips, searching for words to make him understand. "That any other man could make me forget Peter the way you did. When I realized what I'd done, I guess I cried out for Peter's forgiveness. Don't you see?" she pleaded, her eyes glistening. "I won't cheapen Peter's memory because of a moment of foolish weakness. That's why you must forget this thing between us ever happened."

His muttered oath made her wince. She felt his warm hand gather hers up. "I didn't mean to cheapen anything for you, Mrs. McRae," he told her gravely. "If pretending we didn't make love means so damned much to you, then have it your way. Let's get the hell out of here."

Linking his fingers with hers, he tugged her through the tangle of woods. It was a good thing Rule was there to lead. Mandy wasn't watching where she was going with any sound degree of concentration. Most of her mind was struggling with the bittersweet reality of his fingers entwined with hers.

When Rule and Mandy returned to the cottage, Rule silently gathered up Dana and left for the mansion, barely registering his daughter's chatter.

"Daddy." Dana tugged on his little finger.

"Hmmm?" He was hard pressed to drag his thoughts away from the vision of Mandy's glistening nudity, her pink-tipped breasts, her open, pliant lips against his chest. He suppressed a shiver, smiling halfheartedly down at his daughter. "What, honey?"

"I said, Papa Josh didn't make me plant any spinach. We planted cantalopes and watermelons and strawberries." She grinned up at her father, pure, childish joy in her eyes. "I love all those vegetables!"

He grunted with wry humor. "They're the only vegetables you love." Seeing his daughter so happy softened his mood a little, and he swept her up into his arms.

Dragging her stuffed zebra across his shoulder to hug his neck, she asked in a serious little voice, "Did you get hurt in the woods, Daddy? You look like the time when Big Mac kicked you in the tummy."

He was jarred by her question. Was it written all over his face for even a six-year-old child to see? He'd made love to a woman, and she had insisted he forget the best damned experience of his life. So he looked as if he'd been kicked, did he? Hell! Considering everything, he didn't doubt it.

For his daughter's benefit, he shook his head. "I'm just hungry. What about you?"

"Naw." She giggled. "Papa Josh gave me a can of pop and potato chips."

"Oh, fine. The two basic food groups, sugar and preservatives." He tweaked her nose. "And what have I told you about eating that kind of junk?"

She graced him with a sly smile. "Can't 'member."

"Just my luck," he snorted. "Two women, on the same morning, with very selective memories."

When he'd deposited her in the kitchen with Emma, he joined the others in the lavish dining room. The attractively arranged plate went untouched as his mind trailed back to the secret garden. He took a sip of water from his goblet. So he was just supposed to forget everything, was he? Good luck, Danforth, he chided himself acidly.

Bitterness and frustration aside, Rule knew one thing for sure. Luring Mandy into a physical relationship had been selfish, and unlike him. The fact that he'd single-mindedly seduced her was unforgivable. He had no intention of becoming emotionally entangled with anyone, ever again. People may say—even believe—they will love you forever, then the next thing you know their bags are packed and they're walking out the door. Who needs it?

"Good Lord, Danforth, you've cut yourself!" Mr. Perth shouted, breaking through Rule's troubled thoughts.

Glancing down at his hand, he was mildly surprised to see that he'd snapped the stem of his goblet and the jagged end had sliced his hand open. Jetta jumped up and wrapped the torn flesh with her napkin. "That's ugly, Rule. It's going to scar."

His lips twitched with dark irony as he watched the napkin blossom crimson. He clenched his fist. "You could be right," he drawled, not referring to his hand at all.

MANDY BUSIED HERSELF putting away the noon meal's dishes, trying but failing to put Rule's lovemaking from her mind. His hands had roamed with such expertise, his lips had known just how to arouse her, make her body sing with pleasure—

"Mandy?"

Startled, she dropped a plate. It shattered on the wood planking at her feet as she spun around. "What? What is it Papa Josh?" She could feel her face burn and hoped he wouldn't be able to detect her distress.

He hobbled in from the porch, leaning heavily on his cane. A thick, cream-colored envelope was in his free hand. Squinting at her he said, "Land, child. I didn't mean to scare ya. Just thought you'd like to know the yacht's back with the mail. There's a fancy-smancy letter here for ya. Gold and swirly writin' on the envelope." His face creased in a teasing grin. "You expectin' some news from the president?"

She placed a calming hand on her chest and took a deep breath, shaking off her steamy thoughts. "You hold on to it while I clean up this mess. If it's from the president, I doubt if he's spending sleepless hours waiting for my answer." She smiled at him, feeling fairly sure he'd chalked her accident up to everyday clumsiness.

He limped slowly over to the couch and settled into the soft cushions. Plucking his reading glasses from on top of a stack of newspapers, he slid them up his nose. "Says here it's from a—let's see." He drew the envelope close to his face. "Price and Evers—no that's Pierce and Ev—"

"Price and Evans?" Mandy paused, her dust pan poised over the waste basket. "The landscape architect firm in Chicago?"

He scanned it again. "Yep. That's the name."

She dumped the broken china and hurried in to retrieve the envelope from Josh. Tearing it open, she read the letter inside.

"Good news?"

Mandy sat down heavily in the overstuffed chair beside the couch. "They want me to come into the firm as a full partner, Papa Josh." She lifted her eyes from the words, her voice hushed with disbelief.

"That sure is good news."

Mandy folded the letter absently and slid it back into its envelope. She chewed on her lower lip. It was wonderful news. The best news any young landscape architect could possibly get. There just wasn't a more prestigious firm in the country.

"It is good news, ain't it, Mandy?" Josh asked after a drawn-out silence.

She lifted her eyes to meet his as though she were coming out of a trance. "Hmmm?"

Lifting his glasses to rest on his forehead, he frowned at her. "I said, it's good news, ain't it?"

"Oh, yes." She smiled, feeling strangely subdued. "It's . . . it's the most wonderful opportunity. . . ."

Josh pursed his lips thoughtfully. "Well, if this is how you take wonderful news, you'll never get a spot on one o' them game shows where you have to scream and jump up and down for no reason."

"That's very witty, Papa Josh," Mandy observed as she stood. "I guess I'm just not the screaming-and-jumping-up-and-down type."

"You sure that's all it is?"

She forced her gaze to meet his. He was a dear man, but too intuitive for his own good. For some reason, she couldn't completely block Rule's seduction from her thoughts, and it was clouding her happiness over this fantastic job offer. How stupid to let something that was over and done with intrude on her happy news! Squaring her shoulders, she grinned down at her father-in-law and fibbed, "I was just wondering how you'd like Chicago. It's a lot different from Barren Heath Isle."

He waved away her concern with a quivery hand. "Pshaw, woman, don't fret a minute over me. I figure I'll find me a quiet room in an old folks' home. Whittle or somethin'. I won't have you dragging an old man around with ya."

Mandy's smile faded. "Not on your life. An old folks' home, indeed. We're family. We stick together." She planted determined hands on her hips. "Is that understood?"

Josh's yellowed, watery eyes glistened just a little more than usual as he sat there looking up at her. After a minute he lowered his glasses and turned away to thumb through his magazines, grumbling, "You ain't a very bright woman, Mandy McRae. But seein' as how we're family, I guess I'm stuck with ya."

Mandy smiled gently at the top of his bent head. "You're damned right you are, you old cuss."

She felt her spirits lift a little until she remembered that very soon she would have to face Rule. Her stomach lurched at the very thought. How could she ever look him in the eye again?

MEANWHILE, the eager treasure hunters had headed out to renew their search. Having been delayed by Emma's first-aid treatment, Rule was just walking back toward the cottage, Dana in tow, when he heard a loud exchange near the cliff not far away. Since he was not in any great hurry to face Mandy, he changed course to see what all the shouting was about.

As he neared, Rule could see Steppy, Savina and Henry standing on the windy bluff. They were looking over the edge. Rule couldn't see Maybelle, but her whisky voice could be clearly heard, shouting, "Why are you standing there like a wimp, Steppy?"

He bent over. "Just trying to live up to your expectations."

"Oh, shut up and let me have that pickax."

"Don't tempt me, you old—"

"Steppy, don't let her get your goat." Savina knelt and hoisted the ax with both hands, handing it over the edge. "Here, Mrs. Poppy. Is that all?" She sounded irritated.

"I'm off," came the voice.

Rule arrived just in time to see Maybelle, rigged up in rapelling gear, begin to lower herself down the sheer rock face.

"You're off, all right. Off your rocker," Steppy yelled after her, snapping her picture. "But maybe I'm wrong. Who's to say feeble old Lydia didn't rapel down that cliff with the treasure on her back just to throw us off."

Maybelle shook her pickax at him. "Cretin!"

Steppy turned away from the edge, laughing, almost slamming into Henry who was staring dreamily off into space.

"Well, Unk, your face is even more blank than usual this afternoon. Probably just as well, being married to the Dragon Lady and all."

Henry seemed to wake up. "Hello, my boy. . . ." He reached toward his vest pocket, but Steppy grabbed his hand.

"I swear, if you hand me another one of those stupid tickets, I'll hurl myself off this cliff!"

Henry's eyes lit up. "Oh, how excessive!"

Rule chuckled at Henry's appropriate word choice, however accidental.

"But," Henry was continuing, his pudgy face pinched in thought. "Wouldn't that eventually be problematical? I mean, when you hit bottom?"

Steppy groaned theatrically. "It's inspiring the way you grasp things, you crazy old coot."

Savina had been standing in agitated silence slightly behind Steppy during the exchange. She had glanced surreptitiously over at Rule several times, glowering. Finally, she tugged on Steppy's arm. "Let's go, snookie. There's nothing important going on here."

With a grin, he threw his arm around her shoulders and steered her away from the cliff. She pointedly snubbed Rule as they passed him.

"See you later," Rule called, eliciting a wave from Steppy. Savina acted as though he hadn't spoken.

He felt a surge of guilt. He must have really fractured her ego that first day. His lips lifted into a crooked smile. She'd feel avenged if she knew what had happened to him this morning. Mandy had really pummeled his pride—calling out another man's name while she lay in his arms. He gritted his teeth, working at wiping the sound of her passion-racked voice and the vision of her lovely, flushed face from his memory. Sternly he told himself that her rejection had meant nothing more to him than a little injured pride. So she loved another man—a ghost. So what?

"Lovely lady!" Henry gasped, drawing Rule's attention. The tubby man was trotting toward Mandy, who had come partway down the hill from the cabin. When she saw Henry's speedy approach, she stopped, appearing uncertain. She took a couple of tentative steps backward, but Henry leaped toward her, clasping her in his animated embrace. With Mandy clenched to his chest, he bounced her around in a wide circle. After a moment, he relinquished his hold.

Mandy sucked in a breath, her expression perplexed as she watched the addle-minded clown wander off.

Eventually, her glance found Rule's face and stayed. A fitful breeze caught the pale wisps of her hair and molded the thin fabric of her bodice to her breasts. Rule's throat closed at the sight, recalling those breasts teasing his lips. *Damnation, man! Your rutting after this woman has got to stop!* He chafed inwardly. Shifting his gaze to less inflaming sights beyond her shoulder, he called to her, "Hello." He hoped his voice didn't sound as strained to her as it did to him.

Feeling uncharacteristically awkward, he turned to face the ocean. For a long time he stood, gazing at nothing in particular. He heard no answer, nor any rustle of grass to indicate that she was approaching. He could detect nothing of the mild, sweet scent of her, could feel no presence of her skirt brushing intimately yet innocently against his legs. But why the hell should she answer him or even get near him again? She probably feared he'd jump her bones if she got within arm's length. He winced. His stomach crawled with self-loathing. For the first time in his memory, Rule felt like a first-class creep.

Unable to stand the suspense any longer, he turned to look for her, fully expecting her to be gone. She wasn't. He exhaled slowly, grateful for that, at least. She was kneeling, talking to Dana, smoothing curls out of the child's face. She laughed softly. The sound was pleasant to the point of pain against Rule's ears. A moment of silence passed while he struggled with his emotions. When he spoke, his voice was tight. "Could you come here for a minute, Mandy?"

She looked over at him, her smile fading, her expression becoming doubtful.

He spread his arms in mute appeal. "Please."

Turning back to Dana, Mandy said something Rule couldn't hear, then she rose and walked over to him. "Yes?" she asked, meeting his eyes uneasily.

He had the urge to touch her shoulders, but thought better of it. Stuffing his hands in his pockets, he said, "I want to apologize for—"

"Rule, please," she broke in. Her gaze slid to her clenched hands. "I thought we'd promised to forget about that."

"I just don't want things between us to be tense."

She shook her head. Loose wisps of hair flew about her face and shoulders. She looked sweet and fragile but terribly proud. "What's past is past," she whispered, lifting her silvery gaze to meet his again. Sadness and pleading played across her face as she added plaintively, "Rule, we mustn't let this affect our bargain."

"It won't," he assured her.

A trace of relief eased her features as she turned to look out to sea, murmuring, "Thank you."

He looked at her serious, delicate profile for a long moment before she turned back to face him. "Rule?" Her brows were knitted in a thoughtful frown. "Do you think you could talk to Henry—keep him from grabbing me?"

Not terribly surprised that she'd changed the subject, he offered solemnly, "Maybe I'd better work on myself first."

Her eyes widened, but she said nothing. Rule noticed her cheeks had pinkened charmingly before she turned away.

An instant later, a strangled scream was torn from her throat, freezing the blood in his veins.

"Oh my God! Dana!" Mandy rushed to the edge of the cliff and scooped the child up. She'd been sitting on the edge, her legs dangling over the precipice, as she strained to watch her great-aunt far below.

"Sweetheart, you must never go near a cliff. You could fall. Oh, Dana..." She hugged the child. "If *anything* happened to you..."

Dana looked up at Mandy, her eyes shining, her face full of hope. "Do...do you love me, Miss Mandy?"

What was she to say? Seeing Dana in such peril had made her realize that she did love the little girl, almost as though she were her own, but Rule had made her promise. . . .

"I'll take her," Rule cut in, lifting Dana from Mandy's arms. "Of course Miss Mandy is fond of you, Dana. Just like Josh and Emma. They want to be our friends." When his eyes met Mandy's, they were narrowed with concern . . . and something else. Was it a renewed warning for her to keep distance between herself and Dana? Mandy blanched inwardly. Of course it was. She vowed she would try.

"Thank God you saw her," he said finally, but his words had a sharp edge. "I don't know how I could have let that happen."

She pressed her lips together in distress. She knew how it had happened—they'd been so involved in each other.

Deep down, Mandy knew her own recklessness had been in no small part to blame for what had happened in Lydia's secret garden. That's why she'd been on her way down the hill a few moments ago, to make amends. But when she'd actually seen him, she'd gotten cold feet, hesitated.

"You must think I'm a terrible father," he mumbled, drawing her back to the present.

She frowned, denying that emphatically. "I think nothing of the sort. A parent can't keep his eye on a child every—" she faltered, recalling how Josh had tried to comfort her after Rebecca's death with practically the same words; she cleared her throat "—every minute. From what I've seen, you're a good father."

His solemn eyes searched hers, giving her the odd feeling that her private pain had been noted. Slowly his expression regained its warmth, and Mandy found her gaze lost in the depths of noble, brown eyes. "Well, ladies." His glance slid from Mandy to his daughter before he put Dana down. "Are we ready to go treasure hunting?"

Mandy smiled, relieved. Having Dana along would be better, she and Rule would keep a respectable distance with his little girl there. And Mandy promised herself that she would extend that respectable distance to include herself and Dana, for everyone's sake.

When Rule reached for Dana's hand, Mandy noticed the gauze bandage for the first time. Shocked, she asked, "Rule, what happened?"

"Nothing really. It looks worse than it is."

"Daddy broke a glass," Dana supplied, taking his palm and kissing it. "I'm making it better. See?" She smiled adoringly up at her father. "Better, Daddy?"

His eyes were loving as he returned his daughter's smile. "Yes, honey." His gaze shifted to Mandy. "I feel a lot better." The message was soft and welcome. They were once again partners. No, more than that, they were friends. They wouldn't make this morning's rash mistake again.

7

THREE DAYS LATER, Mandy sat mending ZeZe, her thoughts focused on the tiny stitches she was making.

"What are you sewing?" asked Josh as he hobbled in from the porch, leaning heavily on his cane.

"Repairing Dana's comfort object." She looked up and smiled.

He eyed it doubtfully. "Looks like that tired old horse to me."

She laughed. "It's that tired old zebra. She loves it the way Rebecca loved her Raggedy Ann doll. You remember how she dragged that thing—" Her voice faltered. "Well, you remember."

He sat down heavily on the couch, panting weakly. "Mandy?"

She looked back up. "Hmmm?"

"I know you're thirty-two years old, and you probably don't want my nose in your business, but...." He frowned thoughtfully. "Well, here it is. You're not getting too attached to that Danforth man's little girl, are you?"

"Certainly not." Mandy's laugh lacked conviction.

"Well, with all the time you've spent together and that little dress you've been working on, I was just starting to worry that maybe you were gettin' in over your head."

As she cut the thread, she noticed that her fingers were a little shaky. Placing the toy in her lap, she hedged, "What are you getting at?"

He hoisted his thin legs up on the cushions with a grunt. "I'm just saying you've had enough pain in your life. Someday you're gonna have to go your way, and little Dana and her daddy'll go theirs. Don't go learnin' to love her and then have to say goodbye. That's all I'm sayin'."

Mandy chewed on the inside of her cheek for a minute before she ventured, "What about you? Haven't you grown fond of her?"

He picked up his pipe and began to tap tobacco into it. His trembling hands made the job difficult. "I'm an old man, Mandy. Time'll come soon enough when I join my sweet Minna, Peter and little Rebecca. For now, I have you. Way I figure it, I'm lucky." He sucked on the pipe stem, lighting the tobacco before he went on. "As for Dana, she's a sweet child. But she ain't lookin' for a grandpa. She's got a batch of wranglers and a jolly old cook back in New Mexico. Nope." He coughed and cleared his throat before continuing. "What that child's lookin' for is a mama." He squinted over at Mandy. "Worries me some that between what the two've you are lookin' for, you both might end up in a pile of hurt."

She'd heard all this from Rule, and she didn't care to hear it again. Shaking her head at her father-in-law, she hurriedly changed the subject, remarking sternly, "What are you doing with that pipe? Didn't the doctor tell you to quit smoking?"

He raised a sparse brow at her and sucked on his pipe for a moment before he grumbled, "Doc's an old woman. Oh, I know it ain't good for me, but I ain't hurtin' anybody but myself." He wagged the stem at her. "Think about it, Mandy. That little girl ain't no pipe." He clenched the stem between his teeth. "I don't want to see either of you hurtin'."

She turned away to stare out the window. She watched the wind whip the branches of a lone pine for what seemed like a long time before she could voice an answer. "I appreciate your concern, Papa Josh, but I really think I can handle this myself."

He grunted. "Just had to get it out of my craw is all."

She rose and smoothed her skirt. "I understand." Tucking ZeZe under her arm, she headed toward the door. "I said I'd meet Rule and Dana at one o'clock. See you later."

A noncommittal grunt was his only response.

HOURS LATER, Josh having retired, Mandy sat reading, or rather trying to read. Ever since the mistake in the garden, as she chose to think of it, she had been plagued by a nagging, unshakable longing. It haunted her, lurked in the shadows of her every waking thought, prowled beneath the surface of each conversation, every shred of eye contact she shared with Rule.

Every time her hand accidentally brushed his, or their gazes locked unexpectedly, she felt a lush hunger spark to life in the pit of her stomach. It was getting so that she couldn't concentrate on the hunt, and she was constantly berating herself for that. Rule needed the island for his animals, and Josh needed his home. What was the matter with her, anyway? Had she lost her mind? Where was her self-control? Her moral fiber?

What was worse, she knew there was a kindred discontent simmering within Rule. That truly frightened her. The animal magnetism he exuded was dirty pool— cheating—drawing her constantly, making her crave the luxury of his arms again. She didn't like this new, lusty side of Mandy McRae she was seeing, or rather, feeling. She was jumpy, nervous, always on the verge of some crazy swing of emotion—be it a foolishly sensuous elation when he walked into the room or dejection when he walked away.

In a state of high agitation she cast her novel down and leaned back, closing her eyes. She willed herself to relax, to think about nothing. Damn that man's face, anyway. What was it doing in her mind's eye now, taunting, moving toward her with a kiss in those blastedly sexy eyes that promised to burn her to a crisp all the way down to her toes?

Bolting up from her chair, she stormed out onto the porch and dropped into the swing, her gaze flitting over the seascape. She was determined to relax. Inhale! Exhale! Inhale! Ex—what was that? Mandy opened her eyes and strained to hear. There it was again—a rustling in the garden. She stood and crept to the corner of the porch where she had left a whisk broom. She'd teach that pesky rabbit to feast on Josh's tender shoots.

Bent on shooing it away, Mandy sneaked along the exterior wall of the cottage and then leaped around the corner of the house, waving the broom and shouting, "Shoo! Get out! Go 'way, you little pest!"

A frightened shriek stalled Mandy in midstride over a row of beets, and she stumbled to a halt. Dana was cowering amid fledgling tomato plants, her tiny hands thrust before her face. A garden trowel tumbled to the ground in front of her.

"Dana." Mandy dropped her broom and rushed to pick up the little girl. "I'm sorry I frightened you."

Dana curled her arms around Mandy's neck, sniffling. "Why'd you yell at me? You made me scrape my arm," she whimpered, lifting a bloodied elbow for Mandy to examine.

"I didn't mean to yell at you." Mandy kissed her flushed cheek. "I thought you were Old Fatty."

Dana looked up, smudging her cheek with the back of her dirty hand as she wiped away a tear. "Who's Old Fatty?"

"He's a feisty old rabbit that tries to eat Josh's plants. Old Fatty doesn't scare very easily, so I have to shout and act mean to get him to hop off."

Dana sniffed. "If I see Old Fatty, can I pet him?"

Mandy smiled. "He'd love it. He's practically a pet, except during gardening season. Then he's a little pain in the neck." She sat Dana down. "What were you doing out here, anyway? I thought you'd be eating dinner."

"I ate already. Aunt Maybelle came in the kitchen with a big ax and started to dig in the floor. Miss Emma went yelling to that man with the pointy beard, and he told Aunt Maybelle to dig treasure outside. So after I finished eating, I came outside to dig treasure, too."

"Oh, you did, did you?" Mandy laughed. "Does your daddy know where you are?"

Dana shook her curls and whispered, "It's a surprise."

"I'm sure. Well, no problem. I'll take you back to the big house." She took Dana's hand. "First come inside. That elbow needs fixing. And as long as you're here, I've got a surprise I've been saving for you."

"A surprise?" Dana asked, her tear-brightened eyes growing wide at the prospect.

Fifteen minutes later, Dana had a bandaged arm and was wearing the ruffled yellow dress Mandy had made for her. She sat on the edge of the kitchen counter, wagging her bare feet over the side and munching raisin toast. Giggling delightedly, she told Mandy, "Then Aunt Maybelle swung a big black whip at Uncle Steppy and said, 'Back, back, you . . .'" She stopped and raised the toast to tap it against her forehead. "Oh, I can't 'member what name she called him."

Mandy fought a grin. "Probably just as well."

Movement in the corner of her eye made Mandy turn toward the door of the cottage. She was startled to see Rule standing inside, the tension in his face darkening and sharpening his features. His eyes glittered with anger, and something else, a cryptic emotion that was too fragile to name. Yet even without a name, it quickened her pulse. She felt an urgent need to explain. "Rule, we were just about to—"

"Where are your boots, Dana?" he interrupted.

"Hi, Daddy." Completely unaware of the tension crackling in the room, Dana stood up and flounced around on the counter, holding her skirt wide. "Look what Miss Mandy made for me! Isn't it beautiful?" Her face was alight with joy.

Rule's narrowed gaze slowly took in his animated daughter. Ponderous seconds passed before he stated, simply, "Yes, Dana, it's lovely. Now gather up your things. Miss Emma wants to show you how to make brownies."

Mandy lifted Dana down. Nervous to the point of feeling ill, she helped her gather up her jeans, boots and shirt. Then Dana hugged Mandy with a desperate strength, whispering, "It's the best present I ever got. I love you, Miss Mandy."

Mandy swallowed, barely able to hold back tears as she watched the little girl scamper over to her father. He took her clothes from her and bundled them. "Better put on your socks and boots so you don't hurt your feet walking back."

When she had slipped on her boots, he handed her the bundle. "I'll be along in a minute. You go straight to the kitchen. Understood?"

She grinned up at him. "You want me to make you a brownie, Daddy?"

"You'd better. Now scat." He patted her backside, drawing a squeal from her as she clomped out the door and down the steps.

When he turned back to face Mandy, a killing blaze raged in his eyes. Mandy couldn't move, paralyzed by his fury.

Unable to stand the oppressive silence, she implored in a small voice, "It's just a dress, Rule."

He stared at her, his jaw coming alive, leaping and bunching with rage. The air became thick with his unspoken accusations. What was worse, Mandy felt the sting of truth in every spark that sizzled in his eyes. She couldn't blame him for being angry. She knew she had gone too far with the dress. He'd asked her not to draw Dana into a relationship that could hurt his daughter. Hurt them both, really.

But Mandy had allowed her heart to run wildly ahead of her brain. She'd ignored the logic, ignored Rule's warnings and made the dress. If she could only make him understand her motives had been good ones. All she'd wanted was to see delight in Dana's eyes, to give her something that every little girl should have. That was all she'd wanted. But as she stared transfixed into those tortured eyes, she knew that was not all that she had done.

"Congratulations," he growled, his square jaw tight. "Dana loves you—and she'll mourn like hell when you leave her. I hope you're happy."

Mandy was flooded with such a desperate regret that she could no longer meet his gaze. "Oh, Rule," she whispered through a moan. "I'm so sorry, I didn't mean—"

"Maybe you'd like to pretend this never happened, either."

She shuddered and pressed her trembling lips together as he went on, "I'm a grown man. I can survive the fact that you used me in the garden. I'll survive."

She cast him a distressed look. Could he really believe she had used him as he suggested?

"Dana's just a child. How do I tell her you're using her, too?" Angry eyes raked her like talons, drawing fresh blood. His fury was absolute, an unsheathed blade.

"But, Rule—"

"Don't make excuses. I've heard everything from you I want to hear." He ground out the words. "I've arranged with the cook and the housekeeper to give Dana cooking and sewing lessons to keep her occupied." His eyes had grown narrow and hooded. "If you care about her at all, don't try to see her."

His powerful shoulders moved with an air of tremendous fatigue as he turned away. Before Mandy realized it, the door had clicked shut and Rule was gone. With his volatile energy suddenly absent, Mandy lost her strength to stand. She crumbled into a straight-backed chair and dropped her face to her hands. She was bereft, empty, and it was not just because she'd been forbidden to see Dana. The ultimate disaster was that she had betrayed Rule, a man who had been betrayed too many times in his life.

She recalled his eyes, at first heated with the wrath of an erupting volcano, then, freezing over like sleet. His eyes, now cold and unforgiving, had told her that Rule Danforth wanted nothing more to do with her.

Mandy's body quaked as a torrent of sobs escaped. Something—someone—very fine had been ripped from her life, and it was all because of her own foolishness.

FORTY-EIGHT HOURS had dragged by since Rule had walked out of the cottage. He hadn't come by with clues for two days. Mandy hadn't really expected him to, but she had hoped. Now she no longer had hope to cling to. She sawed out the final stanza of "Flight of the Bumblebee" and then stuffed her violin in its worn case.

She'd taken lonely refuge on the rocky beach below the cottage over an hour ago, playing her heart out, hoping the screeching concert would serve as a sort of penance and drain her of her nagging guilt. It hadn't worked. Her ire at herself was more acute than ever. How could she have done such a selfish thing? How could she have put Dana in a position of being so badly hurt?

She hoisted the case and headed toward the incline that led up to the bluff. She'd come to a decision during the long, punishing recital. She would apologize. She must convince Rule to allow her to continue to help him. Their partnership was too important to allow it to flounder now.

The afternoon was dying a fiery death, matching Mandy's mood. Rule would probably be heading back to the mansion for dinner soon. She decided to head in that direction. Maybe she'd run into him. With resolution lifting her chin and trepidation fluttering in her stomach, Mandy picked her way up the rocky slope. When she reached the crest of the trail, she collided with Steppy, who was just rounding an ancient, gnarled oak.

"Whoa!" Steppy grasped her elbow to steady her. "Don't fall all the way back down. Be messy." He grinned down at her. "Say, is everything okay down there? Sounded like babies screaming."

It took all of Mandy's willpower not to giggle hysterically. This was not her day! She patted her violin case. "No babies. Just my gift for music. Most people think I'm torturing cats."

Steppy looked sheepish. "Oops. Sorry. Guess I'm no judge of music."

She leaned against the oak. "Don't worry about it. Next time it'll probably sound like tortured cats to you, too." She smiled wanly.

He chuckled, shaking his head. "You're a good sport."

"As a violinist, I'm a good sport," Mandy smiled sadly, wanting to change the subject. She asked, "How's the hunt going?"

Steppy shrugged, heaving a sigh with it. "Who knows? With Lydia's crazy clues, the treasure might as well be on the moon." He shifted a manila envelope from one hand to the other. "I'm taking a break. Maybelle's been driving me and Savi nuts. She's gone to take a couple of aspirin, and lie down—Savi, not Dracula's daughter. Anyway, I thought I'd look for a quiet spot to gather my thoughts. Then I heard . . . well, you know."

"Tortured babies."

Steppy shook a finger at her. "Now, now, I just said screaming."

Mandy laughed in spite of her mood. "Either way, the beach is quiet enough now." Looking idly at the envelope, she asked, "What have you got there?"

"Oh—uh, just some of my pictures. Developed 'em last night."

"Here?"

"Yeah. Savi showed me Arnold's darkroom. Great equipment. Seems he dabbled in photography when he wasn't making millions inventing things."

Mandy was surprised. She hadn't known about the darkroom. She mused wryly that perhaps Rule didn't make his best deal by accepting her help. Then she

winced. He wasn't exactly in hot pursuit of her suggestions at the moment. She tried to shrug off that thought,
asking, "What are you going to do with the photographs on the beach?"

"Thought I'd go through 'em. I want to make up a
portfolio of my work. Maybe show 'em to somebody
someday about a job or something." He ran a hand
through what there was of his hair and sighed. "Or I
might just make sailboats out of 'em and sail them toward China. Who knows?"

Mandy was curious. "May I see them?"

A rather charming blush crept up his neck as he insisted, "They aren't very good."

"I'll bet they are."

Hesitantly, he handed her the envelope, muttering,
"Okay, but it's your funeral."

"You're too modest," she offered gently, pulling out
the eight-by-ten color photos. She could feel Steppy's
intent stare as she slowly thumbed through them.
Among others, there was a close-up of a ladybug on a
dewy leaf, a sparkling spider web with a bat, its wings
spread in flight behind it, silhouetted by a striking ma-
genta sunset. Finally there was one particularly amazing shot of Maybelle. Stern, angular and willful, her
face was captured within a wispy ring of dark smoke.
There was something riveting in her eyes that leaped
from the page, physically threatening.

"Why, Steppy, these are wonderful. Especially Maybelle."

He laughed nervously. "Thanks. I call that one 'Evil
Incarnate.'"

"You going to try to sell these?"

He shook his head. "Nah. I don't have the talent."

Mandy took another look at the photos. "Mind if I
try something?"

He squinted, skeptical. "What?"

"One of my first clients was Ward Jamison. You may have heard of—"

"The wildlife photographer?" he blurted, animated with excitement. "He's one of my all-time idols. You *know* him?"

She slid the photos back in the envelope. "Well enough to get his opinion on these. What do you say? Do I have your permission to send them to him?"

Steppy clapped her on the shoulders. "Do you *ever!* Thanks. I'd be crazy not to want that man's opinion. You're blue chip, Mandy."

"It's my pleasure." She flinched, wishing Steppy would take it a little easier with his enthusiasm.

As they headed away from the bluff, Steppy shook his head and exhaled loudly. "My dad always said taking pictures like this was strictly for sissies. He forced me into the car business with him. When he died, I loused it up royally. Lost everything." He made a disgusted sound. "Dad always said I was a lazy dreamer, and I'd never amount to a pile of dented hubcaps. Guess he was right. Just look at me."

Mandy smiled kindly. "Dads aren't always the best judges of their sons' abilities." He glanced at her, surprise in his eyes. "Listen, Steppy, the world would be a dull place if everybody went into the car business. I have a feeling your talents just don't lie in that area."

He laughed tartly. "Neither does Maybelle. She says my talents don't even lie on this planet."

Mandy looked away, not wanting to say anything unkind about his aunt, but hating what the older woman's barbs had done to his sense of self-worth. She turned back to look at him. "You know what they say, you're never a hero in your own family. I wouldn't worry about Maybelle."

He tugged on her braid like a playful third-grader. "Maybe you ought to give up the violin and take up psychology."

"That's about the nicest way anybody's every suggested I give up the violin."

They shared a companionable smile.

She tapped the envelope. "I'll let you know what Ward says."

With a hearty goodbye, Steppy went off to dinner. Mandy looked around. Rule was nowhere to be seen. Sighing despondently, she headed back to the cabin to get Josh's dinner on. She was glad she'd been able to lighten Steppy's load a little, but there was still the matter of a huge apology she owed Rule. She promised herself she'd catch him the first thing tomorrow.

MANDY THREW OFF her covers and swung her legs over the side of the bed. Fumbling for her clock radio, she turned it toward her. It was only eleven-thirty. Impossible! It felt as if she'd been squirming and fretting half the night instead of just one hour. Gritting her teeth in a defiant determination to get some sleep, she slid back under the covers and clamped her eyes shut. She must rest. She'd barely closed her eyes in two nights. Rule's face kept struggling to the forefront of her thoughts, looming there, those cursed eyes brooding. She rolled over onto her stomach with a groan.

Something scraped at the window. "Oh, that's just great," she muttered into her pillow. Now a branch was going to rub back and forth against her window screen all night, providing additional mental torture. She didn't see why some evil foreign power didn't come in and stick splinters under her fingernails just for the practice. She wasn't going to get any sleep, anyway.

There it was again. She frowned, baffled. This time the sound was more like knocking. Branches didn't knock. Besides—she grew alert—there wasn't a trace of wind.

"Miss Mandy?" came a tiny, disembodied voice.

She sat up. Good Lord, it was Dana! Hurriedly pulling on her terry robe, she scurried to the window and tugged it open. "Dana," she whispered, her voice strained with worry, "What are you doing out there?"

She looked so small peering up at Mandy, her eyes big and round, reflecting the moon in their depths. "I—I just wanted to see you," she whimpered, her teeth chattering with the chill.

"Come around to the porch," Mandy called quietly as she grabbed up a quilt and hurried to the front of the cabin.

Seconds later she'd pulled Dana up, bundling her on her lap in the swing. "Bare feet?" Mandy chastised with a wan smile.

"I didn't want to wake Daddy," Dana whispered, snuggling against the softness of Mandy's chest. "I put on the dress you made me, did you see?"

Mandy nodded. "Yes, but you shouldn't have come out so late. The island can be dangerous—there are caves and cliffs—many places you could fall in the dark and get hurt."

Dana looked up, her face brightening with excitement. "Oh, I heard of caves. They go inside the ground. Show me a cave, Miss Mandy!"

Though Mandy felt a warm comfort holding the child in her arms, she knew she should send her immediately home. Yet, swinging there in the fragrant night, she couldn't quite let her go. Just for a moment, she promised herself.

The moon illuminated the rocky shore and cliff near the mansion. Mandy pointed to a gaping black opening near where the surf was pounding the beach. "Over there. See that black hole in the wall of rock?"

Dana craned her head around and nodded. "Is that a cave?"

"Yes. And someday I'll take you—I'll ask your father to take you there. But it's too dangerous at night." Smoothing Dana's hair, she added in a melancholy whisper, "We'd better get you back to bed."

Dana's face clouded, and she clung to Mandy's neck all the way down the path to the mansion's kitchen entrance. "Can you get yourself up to bed?"

Dana nodded, her expression still hangdog as Mandy lowered her to her feet and removed the blanket from around her.

Mandy squatted beside her and lifted her chin. "Promise me you won't go sneaking out at night anymore."

Dana didn't say anything for a minute, and Mandy could see some of her father's stubbornness in the child's face. Finally, in a tremulous little voice, she promised. With one final, desperate hug, Dana relinquished Mandy and padded into the darkened mansion.

Mandy watched the door for a long time after Dana had disappeared. After a while her legs began to ache from their cramped position. Pushing up, she turned away, feeling hollow and sad. She pictured Dana's crestfallen face and tears clouded her eyes. The child was just as forlorn that they must be separated as she. And the unhappy situation was all Mandy's doing. She uttered a sharp curse and cringed at the nasty taste it left in her mouth.

THERE HE WAS, heading toward the woods. Mandy's heart hammered against her ribs in nervous anticipation. She jumped off the porch and started after him, practically running. "Rule..." She puffed his name in a hoarse whisper, not sure if it was fatigue or fright that made her mouth so cottony.

He turned, his face stern, cautious.

"Rule." She waved. "Please... *wait*."

- When she reached him, she could see suspicion in his eyes. He said nothing.

She swallowed, searching valiantly for the right words. Her insides were shot through with splinters of dread. "Rule, I... Please forgive me. I'm sorry for what I've done to you—and to Dana. Don't shut me out. Let me help you. Remember we made a bargain. I'll do anything you say, just... just let me help...." It had all come out in a rush. To her ears it had sounded garbled and stupid. She wrung her hands.

He just stood there, regarding her with narrowed eyes. He was so intimidatingly tall and broad that she found herself taking a step back. She didn't like him towering over her, it made her anxious, and far too aware of him. She willed herself to say nothing more, to stand as proud and as tall as she could and wait him out. It was up to Rule now.

Skepticism hung in his gaze as he muttered, "Help me? That's very funny, coming from you."

The naked pain of his words stung her heart, and she could find no reply.

His lips lifted in a smile that held no mirth. "As far as any so-called bargain goes, don't tell me you're sticking to that tired story of trying to help Josh?"

"But it's true," she pleaded, grabbing his hands in reckless abandon. "Every word, I swear."

"Cut it out," he gritted, but he didn't pull away from her grasp.

Taking advantage of that infinitesimal softening, she clutched his hands to her chest, imploring, "Rule, give me another chance. You need this island, and I really might be a help in getting it for you—if you give me the chance." Mandy swallowed miserably, fighting tears. "Rule, you're Dana's father. That gave you the right to say everything you said the other night. I—I was wrong."

His frown began to ease as his eyes roamed her stricken face. After a silent moment, he pulled from her grasp, framing her blazing face with callused hands. Exhaling raggedly, he said, "We've both got some heavy emotional baggage to deal with. I was pretty rough on you the other night." His fingers were cool and strong against her skin, his voice almost gentle.

"Then we're partners again?" she asked, an uncertain smile hovering about her lips.

Dropping his hands from her face, he tangled his fingers loosely in hers. "I suppose."

"And Dana?"

She sensed more than saw a stiffening in his jaw. "With Emma's cooking lessons and Maggie's sewing lessons, she'll be a very busy girl from now on." He turned away to follow the path, pulling her in his wake.

Mandy tugged at her lower lip, wondering if she should tell Rule about his daughter's late-night visit, then decided against it. She didn't want to stir up more trouble between them. But she promised herself if it happened again, she would have to say something. She looked around, wondering where she was being dragged at such a rapid clip. "Where are we going?"

"Where there are 'Walls where no walls stand.'"

"Today's clue?"

He nodded. "What does it suggest to you?"

Except for the sound of the rustling grass beneath their feet, they walked in silence while Mandy thought. Finally, when she realized where they were heading, she stumbled to a halt, murmuring hesitantly, "The secret garden?"

He paused and turned to face her. "We didn't get much searching done the last time we were there." The barest hint of a challenge glinted in his eyes. "I won't force you to go if the idea frightens you."

He watched her closely, and she knew he expected her to back down and run like a frightened child. His fingers barely held hers. It would have been easy to free herself, easy to turn tail. After all, he knew where the garden was; there was no reason for them both to go. She could rightfully suggest that she'd save them time by looking somewhere else. Her eyes flitted behind Rule to the looming woods and then back to his face. One of Rule's well-formed brows lifted in mute question.

She fought off a quiver of yearning to feel, again, the hard muscles of his back. His hips. The soft tangle of hair that furred his chest. With a mighty effort, she forced her desire to a back shelf in her mind.

Squaring her shoulders, she assured him quietly. "Of course, I'll go. We're . . . partners, aren't we? It's just a garden," she murmured, trying to convince herself. "You and I can go back there and be perfectly cool, rational human beings. We're mature adults. We don't have to rut like . . . Well, like whatever animals rut."

"Wild asses," he offered.

She sniffed disdainfully. "Why doesn't that surprise me?"

A pleasant sound rumbled in his throat and his eyes began to twinkle. Shaking his head, he turned back to the trail.

"I'd like to know what you think is so funny," she said. But it didn't really matter. The important thing was that Rule was smiling.

8

"NOTHING . . ." Mandy sighed, dropping down tiredly on the bed of silver ground cover. She stretched her legs out into the circle of sunshine that poured through the bright, open halo above the garden. The sun caressed her calves, making them appear milky white, trim and strong. She smoothed her skirt down below her knees, but not before Rule had an excellent view of one shapely thigh. She felt more than heard his approach as he sat down in the deep shade not far away.

She turned to look at him, working to keep her mind on business. "I was sure there'd be something wonderful here."

"I could comment, but I won't." He drew up a knee and hooked an arm around it.

Her eyes searched the smoldering embers in his, and she swallowed uncomfortably. The fragrant place brought back all too clearly the memory of their recently shared love, quickening their awareness of each other to a point where it was becoming difficult to ignore.

Mandy inwardly collected herself, searching for a safe subject. "Did I tell you about my job offer?"

His eyes narrowed. "No, you didn't."

"A landscape architect firm in Chicago, Price and Evans. Very prestigious." He didn't comment. Clearing her throat, she hurried on. "There was a short article about one of my projects in *Architectural Digest* magazine just before my family—" She paused, unable to finish the sentence. "Anyway, apparently the story made a ripple."

"Congratulations." Rule's face was sober, his expression unreadable.

"Thanks. I—I'll be a partner. It's a wonderful opportunity. It's just Josh I'm worried about. Chicago is so big. I don't know how he'll deal with such a culture shock."

She stood abruptly, brushing fretfully at her skirt. Her body was so pricked through with nervousness that she felt she'd better keep moving or she'd explode. "Maybe we ought to be getting back."

He was standing very near when she looked up. "Have you given up on us?" he asked near her ear.

"Us?" Her voice was unsteady. Why did his scent have to invade her mind, cloud her thinking?

"Finding Lydia's treasure."

"Oh . . ." Turning toward him, she lifted her chin without conscious thought, a mute invitation for a kiss. The need to feel his mouth full against hers was too strong to fight any longer. Deliberately, she leaned forward until her breasts pressed against his chest. She lifted parted lips and moved them slowly, warmly across his.

She curled her arms around his neck, her fingers eager to know the hard heat of his shoulders and back. With a moan, Rule responded, his splendid mouth becoming insistent, his tongue thrusting. Delighting sensitive recesses of her mouth, he drew her deeper and deeper into his seductive spell.

His hard, muscular chest was warm, even through the layers of clothing, and Mandy knew a wild desire to rip the damnable fabric away. She could feel the heavy thudding of his heart, while hers pounded with a frantic rhythm of its own. Pressing herself firmly to him, she gasped to feel his arousal throbbing intimately against her, and her own core began to pulsate with a wild need.

A tremor quaked through Rule. Without warning, he lifted his face from hers, growling out a low curse. With what seemed like terrific effort, he retreated from her, his face stark as he turned away. "Dammit, woman, what the hell did you do that for?"

"Me?" she managed weakly, her breathing labored.

He spun back around, his eyes blazing. "Hell yes, you. You make such a big point of our being partners, then you lie down in a bed of flowers showing just enough leg, you come on with those innocent eyes. Then, wham! A kiss that could singe asbestos." He grinned sardonically. "I know I told you I was a big boy and I'd survive being used. But, lady, you keep this up, and I may just do a little using myself—Peter or no Peter. I'm no ghost, Mandy. I'm flesh and blood. Or hadn't you noticed?"

His accusation stung. Shuddering, she drew an uneven breath, feeling confused and guilty. What was wrong with her? She raised stricken eyes to meet his, which held the wounded, distrustful look of a loyal dog, beaten for no reason. Unprepared to deal with the situation, Mandy backed away. Mumbling an apology, she stumbled out of the garden and ran blindly from him.

LATE AFTERNOON SUN streamed into the living room through arched fanlights and French doors. Rule tried to convince himself he was comfortable in the paisley-covered armchair. He wasn't succeeding. He took in the grandeur of the room. It reeked of money, from the carved marble mantel to the scattering of highly polished antiques, including the rosewood coffee table he had to keep squelching the urge to rest his boots on.

Rocking his head back, he eyed the domed ceiling, gritting his teeth against another curse, one of many he'd blasted himself with since Mandy had stumbled from the garden. He was disgusted for his outburst. The kiss that was ripping at his guts had been just as much his fault as hers. He hadn't been forced at gunpoint to drag her along with him in the first place.

"Hi there, Cowboy," a sexy voice purred, drawing Rule from his dark reverie. He turned toward the sound. Jetta was standing before a wall of bookshelves, grinning at him. In shorts and halter top, his buxom cousin made a fetching sight. She asked, "Why aren't you out treasure hunting?"

He shrugged. "Lack of inspiration. What about you?"

"Oh, honey, I'm still hunting." She climbed gracefully up the library ladder. On tiptoe, she began to pull dusty books down one at a time, flipping through pages. "I had a flash that 'Walls where no walls stand' might mean fiction—maybe a key to a treasure chest is taped in a book. What do you think? Really dumb?"

Rule laced his fingers together beneath his chin. "Sounds as plausible as anything I've come up with today. Good hunting."

She winked and turned away from him, replaced the book and grabbed the next.

"What have you seen of Gavin lately?"

The room echoed with her throaty laughter. "Not enough. He's afraid I'll worm something out of him, so he makes himself scarce after breakfast."

"Probably very wise of him," Rule remarked without inflection. He only wished he were half as bright as far as Mandy was concerned. With a twisted smile,

Rule wondered if he wouldn't be better off taking cooking lessons with his daughter than spending so much time with a desirable woman who spent her love on flowers and ghosts.

"Wise, nothing. Old Gavie may be a flirt on the surface, but underneath the old poop's a nervous coward with a possessive wife who's got him on a very short leash. She calls him twice a day. Can you imagine?"

Rule grinned at her back. "No doubt she's seen your picture."

Jetta turned to look at him with wide, innocent eyes that were almost convincing. "Now, Rule. You don't think I'd stoop to pillow talk to find the treasure, do you?"

He grinned. "Perish the thought."

"Lydia chose well when she picked hen-pecked ol' Gavie," she admitted with a throaty giggle. "Guess I'll have to rely on my brains."

"Into every life a little rain . . ."

"Oh, you." Jetta winked again and returned to her work.

"Daddy?"

Rule was startled to realize Dana had come in and was standing silently at his elbow. She was wearing the yellow dress Mandy had made for her. She barely allowed it off her back long enough for it to be washed and ironed. "What is it, sweetheart?" His smile was weary.

"Can I go see Miss Mandy now? Miss Emma said dinner won't be till the fat hand is on the six." She pointed to the mantel clock. "It's only on the four, Daddy."

Rule took her hand in his. "No, Dana. I've told you Miss Mandy is a busy woman. Now run on to your room and play with ZeZe. I'll be in after a while."

Dana's lashes swooped down to hide dejected eyes. "Okay, Daddy," she whispered, shuffling out of the room.

As Rule watched his little girl's retreat, his jaw tightened. She was so small, so unhappy, so innocent of any wrongdoing and suffering so much. He opened his mouth, weakening in his resolve, ready to call her back, to tell her she was free to find Mandy and enjoy whatever little time they might have together. But before the words were out, he realized that giving in to his guilt would do neither Mandy nor Dana any real good. It was better this way in the long run—keep things from getting any worse than they already were.

He leaned back and closed his eyes, exhaling tiredly. He felt lousy. In trying to protect his daughter, he'd made her miserable, and made himself feel lower than a snake in a ditch. He snorted his disgust, drawing Jetta's attention.

"What?" she called. "Did you say something, Rule?"

He didn't bother opening his eyes, just moved his head from side to side. "No, ma'am. Just over here calling myself names."

Jetta's laughter wafted across the room. "It's been one of those days, huh?"

He scowled up at the ceiling. His mind's eye rebelliously refused to dismiss the images of two very unhappy females from his brain—one his daughter, the other his . . . partner. Gruffly he told Jetta, "Yep. You could say it's been one of those days."

MANDY SCRAMBLED up from her quilt for the tenth time and walked into the lapping tide. She was as restless as the ocean water that was sliding back and forth across the cove. She dug her toes into the sand and kicked a glob of the stuff high. A gust of wind caught it and blew it back into her face. She gasped and spat, wiping her eyes. "Great," she muttered. "Mandy McRae, you're your own worst enemy! How many other people can kick sand in their own faces and totally alienate men just by kissing them!"

"What?"

At the sound of Rule's voice Mandy spun around, her face flaming with embarrassment. When she saw how far away he was, she realized he couldn't have heard her. "Oh . . . hello . . ." She breathed the words through a sigh of relief, backing up until the water tickled and ebbed around her calves. Self-consciously she tugged on her cutoffs, wishing she wasn't wearing shorts. She had trouble enough dealing with Rule Danforth fully clothed.

The half moon was yellow and low in the sky behind him. He ambled toward her, a lanky silhouette, looking terribly masculine in his snug jeans, Western hat and boots. He had an easy, fluid gait that became almost hypnotic as he took each unhurried step across the sand.

She couldn't see his face, couldn't tell his mood. She wondered if he felt as tense as she did. He certainly wasn't walking like a man on tenterhooks. She bit her lip realizing the folly of that idea. After all, hadn't he pushed her away that afternoon?

"Were you talking to me?" he asked, when he reached the quilt.

She shook her head. "No. Just to myself." She winced at the idiocy of her remark.

He mumbled something that Mandy couldn't quite hear. It sounded a little like "You, too?"

She asked, "What was that?"

He shook his head. "Nothing. If I were you, I'd stick to the violin. Men in white coats cart off people who mumble to themselves."

He seemed to be in a fine mood. That knowledge served only to blacken Mandy's. She turned away to watch the stars twinkle merrily in the heavens, unconcerned with her turmoil. "I'll keep that in mind," she promised glumly.

"May I sit?"

"Go ahead." Water splashed her knees and she stifled a shiver. The temperature was dropping rapidly. If she had any sense, she'd march right back to the cottage to change. But for some demented reason, even in her state of high anxiety, she didn't want to leave. She turned back. He'd taken off his hat and was sitting there, his arms drawn around one knee, watching her. When his hat was off, she could see his features in the moonlight. He wasn't smiling, but he wasn't exactly frowning. He was just . . . watching.

They looked at each other for a long time. It was an odd experience, much less threatening than she would have guessed, considering how angry he had been this afternoon.

Before either of them broke the silence, their attention was attracted to a bouncing beam of light off to Mandy's left. They turned to see Maybelle heading toward them along the beach, a heavy-duty flashlight in one hand and a metal detector in the other. She was oblivious to Mandy and Rule until she almost tripped over Rule, and her detector burst into a loud hum.

"What the—" She stumbled back. "Oh, it's *you!* Young man, just what do you think you're doing out here in my way?" Righting her pith helmet, she clunked herself in the eye with her flashlight and cursed.

Rule stood up and relieved her of her detector, turning it off. "Sorry, Aunt Maybelle, it was my fault. I shouldn't have been cluttering up the beach with my body."

"My detector went crazy. What have you got on you, anyway?"

"Belt buckle. Sorry about that."

She grabbed the detector from him. "I'll *bet* you're sorry! Just because you're Arnold's son doesn't mean you have any more right to the money than I do. And don't think I haven't anticipated sabotage! I'm watching you, boy." She slid a damning look toward Mandy. "And you, you interloper." Waving her flashlight, she called over her shoulder. "Come, my sweet. They did us no real harm."

A few paces back Henry was hurrying toward them, his trusty salad fork held high like a beacon in the darkness. "Coming my little potato bug!" he chirped, waving pleasantly at Mandy and Rule as he skipped by.

When they were well away along the beach, Mandy eyed heaven helplessly and quipped, "Maybelle's on to us, Rule."

Mimicking a movie gangster, he said, "Guess we'll have to dump our plot to sabotage Henry's fork."

Laughter gurgled in Mandy's throat. She felt better for some strange reason. Seeing the bizarre couple had the same effect as one might expect from sitting on a whoopie cushion—startling some of the tension out of her. Wading out of the water, where she was turning blue, she joined Rule on the quilt.

Determined to keep the conversation light, Mandy asked, "Why are you out on the beach so late without your trenching fork?"

"Shows a real lack of foresight, I know."

She smiled inwardly at his dry wit but said nothing. In the silence that followed, she began to pat her wet legs dry with the edge of the quilt.

"What about you?"

His question took her by surprise. What could she say? *You make me feel so damned squirrelly, so damned foolish and guilty, I had to get away!* No way would she say that. Not even if her life depended on it. She leaned back on one elbow and faced him, telling him a half-truth. "I like the night. It's calming."

"You nervous?"

She blanched. Must he hit the nail on the head so directly? She looked up at the stars. Some winked, some blinked, some stared blankly. No help at all. She stuttered, "I...that was just a figure of speech." Sitting back up to put distance between herself and his glittering eyes, she asked, out of the blue, "You said someday you'd tell me how you got into saving endangered zebras and wi—whatever." She wasn't going to say wild asses, but she wasn't sure why not.

"I said it was a long, dull story."

She looked over at him, serious. "Nothing so worthwhile could be dull, Rule. Tell me."

He turned away, looking out to sea. Or was he looking far beyond that? Perhaps years away? She watched his profile, enjoying the moonlit view of his angular, pensive features.

After a moment, he picked up a shard of broken shell and fingered it, saying, "My mother cooked at a little diner in Albuquerque. We lived in two rooms upstairs. Every day, an equine veterinarian who worked at the Rio Grande Zoological Park came in for lunch. His name was Jeb Smiley." Rule tossed the shell into the water. "When my mother died, Doc Smiley took me in, gave me a room, a job cleaning the animals' habitats, and taught me to love animals as he did." He looked over at Mandy, catching her by surprise with a wry smile. "If you ever need a lion's habitat cleaned, I'm your man."

She grinned. "I'll remember. Please go on."

He lifted a skeptical brow, as though he didn't think she could really be interested. Turning away, he began again. "Doc was a frail old man. He had a bad liver and a good dream. He wanted to build a propagation center for highly endangered equids. A refuge filled with technological wizardry to help dying species flourish and grow. But he died too soon—the day I graduated from veterinary school." He shrugged. "At least he lived long enough to know I'd take it from there."

"Now you're living out Doc's dream for him," Mandy supplied quietly.

He turned to look at her, his lips curving upward just slightly. "It's my dream, too."

She found herself smiling back. "So you're *Doctor* Danforth. You never told me."

He grinned. "Would you have let me treat your hip if I had?"

She felt a blush rush up her neck and scorch her cheeks. Thankful for the darkness, she murmured, "Good point." Floundering for a subject that would take her mind off his hands doing anything to her hips, she hurried on, "I heard a quote in a botany class once, about when a form of life becomes extinct. It went something like 'Another heaven and another earth must pass before...'" She frowned, unable to recall the rest.

"'... before such a one can come again,'" he finished-for her. He smiled outright, his teeth glistening, making the hair on her nape stand erect. "William BeBee said it. I guess I shouldn't be surprised that you'd know a quote from an obscure naturalist, being in the business you're in. Still I'm impressed."

"Thank you." She turned away, quelling a delightful shiver that had nothing to do with the evening's chill. "'Another heaven and another earth' is a poetic way to describe the tragedy of extinction."

"A tragedy that is always with us. One species of living things dies out every day."

She turned back to face him. "Every day?"

When he nodded, she whispered, "That's unbelievable."

"Unfortunately, too many people think that way. They don't believe whales could ever disappear even though they're indiscriminately slaughtered, or that the oyster is being killed off by pollution. Any number of species of plant and animal life could one day simply be gone if we don't do something about it now." He shut his eyes, sounding weary. "I don't intend for my animals to be among the missing."

Mandy didn't know when she'd been as touched as she felt by Rule's quiet words. She had a tremendous urge to take his broad shoulders into her arms and hug him, hold him, tell him his dream would come true if she had anything to say about it. But recalling this afternoon's disaster in the garden, she stifled her urge almost completely. As a compromise, she squeezed his hand, exclaiming, "Me neither. Let's go." Grabbing his hat, she plopped it on his head.

"What? Where?" he asked as she jumped up and began to drag the quilt up even as he sat on it.

"The cave. Let's look there again. It has walls that aren't really walls. We haven't any time to waste. If Maybelle can keep searching at night, why can't we?"

Adjusting his hat so that he could see, he stood up, reminding her, "It's dark in there."

"Never fear. As a girl, I was a Bluebird." Her little blue flashlight rolled off the quilt and thudded into his foot. He scooped it up and flicked it on. Its weak circle of yellow light wasn't encouraging. He glanced sideways at her, his expression skeptical. "I think we'd be better off if you'd been a bat."

They'd been in the cavern the first week, but had found nothing. Why they were there again, in the pitch dark with a flashlight that could have been rivaled by a flaming book of matches, was anybody's guess.

"I have a gut feeling about this place," Mandy explained in a whisper. She always found it eerie to hear her own words echo back to her and tried to avoid it.

"What do your guts say about these flashlight batteries? Do we have a chance in hell of finding our way back out?"

She waited until his words had ceased bouncing off the dripping walls before she peered up at him and said, "If you're afraid, you can wait outside."

He chuckled. The sound echoed around her, deep and rich.

She aimed her flashlight toward the floor. It was pitted with holes, some no bigger than marbles, some large and filled with water. He took her elbow and helped her as they picked their way around the uneven surface, heading deeper into the grotto. The air smelled dank and cold.

She shone the flashlight along the carved and fluted walls. Glistening flecks of crystal deposits blinked back like cats' eyes glowing in the darkness. It gave her a queer feeling of being watched.

They walked for about ten minutes over the precarious surface before the ground flattened out. They were now deep inside the cave. No longer could they hear the sound of waves breaking against the rocks outside; it was deathly still, but for the occasional sound of fluttering wings. Mandy's flesh crawled, knowing that not far above their heads, small, gray bats hung in hairy clusters. She reminded herself that bats ate insects. They did not, as Emma kept insisting, fly into your hair and make you go crazy. Nevertheless, she kept her light directed away, not caring to disturb them any more than necessary.

"What do your guts say now?" Rule asked, making Mandy jump and drop her quilt.

"What?"

"I'm sorry. I didn't mean to frighten you," he remarked through a chuckle as he picked up the quilt for her.

She swallowed, calming herself. "You didn't frighten me," she lied. "I was just startled for a second. Uh—" She motioned toward the floor. "Would you mind spreading it out. I'd like to rest my bruised feet and think."

When they were both seated, he asked, "Would you like me to rub them for you?"

She declined with a nervous laugh. "Don't be silly, Rule, I—"

"I'm a doctor, remember." He took one frigid foot in his warm hands and began to work such wonders that her argument melted into a sigh of relief.

"Did they teach you that in veterinary school?"

He laughed. "No, but thanks. The closest I get to a compliment from my patients is a boisterous nudge between the shoulder blades."

Mandy leaned back on her elbows, noticing idly that the beam of her flashlight was growing weaker. She hoped it would last, but couldn't become too panic-stricken about it at this particular moment. She had one foot in heaven.

"Rule," her mind ambled down a wayward trail, and she lazily allowed it to roam. "Why did your wife leave you?"

His hands stilled for only a fraction of a second, but Mandy noticed it. She bit the inside of her cheek. Why had she asked such a personal question? "Never mind," she added hurriedly. "That's none of my business."

His massage continued, firm and healing. She could not see his face well because the flashlight was lying on the blanket. Unfortunately, she had an unsettling view of his lap as he sat there, nestling her foot on a muscled thigh. She was about to suggest that they leave when he spoke.

"Peggy knew I planned to try and build a propagation center, but I guess she always thought she could get me to change my mind. She wanted me to set up a practice in Kentucky where her father had a fancy horse-breeding business. She had it all figured out—wealthy clients, big house, grand social life like the one she grew up with. When she finally realized I never would, she left. End of story."

"She left Dana just like that?"

He let out a long, slow breath. "I still can't believe that, but we haven't heard from her since the day she walked out—except when I was served the divorce papers."

He brought her other foot up to rest on his thigh. Mandy couldn't help but notice how close it was to his groin. She could feel the radiant heat of him. In the enclosed space of the narrowing cavern, she became very aware of his scent. It was warm in the cold air, beckoning to her like the scent of a freshly baked mince pie cooling on a windowsill. She felt like a hungry vagabond, close enough to sniff, but without the right to taste.

Forcing herself to put her mind on safer ground, she asked, "Do you hate them—your father and your ex-wife?"

He stopped massaging and rested a hand on her ankle. It felt nice there. "Be a waste of time," he murmured. "Besides, they taught me about the frailty of relationships."

"I thought there could be nothing worse than having someone you love die," Mandy mused in a whisper. "I can't imagine how terrible it must be to have someone you love walk out on you."

Mandy couldn't see it. She couldn't hear it, but it was unmistakably there, palpitating in the darkness. Pain. Rule's pain. Harsh, desperate and crushing, it was swelling up like a bad bruise and filling the cavern. Her unthinking remark had cut him deeply, yet his only physical reaction to her words was to turn his face slightly away. That, at least, she could see. "Oh, Rule, what a *foolish* thing for me to say," she cried.

To make amends, she pulled her legs up and knelt, taking his face in her hands. "But even I could never be as foolish as Arnold and Peggy were, when they walked away from someone as fine and caring as you."

His eyes were glittering when they met hers. She couldn't tell if he was angry at her or stinging with the hurt of her words. She felt terrible for having brought up the subject. But even so, she was glad she knew where he stood. Life had dealt Rule Danforth an unfair hand, yet he had come through it with admirable strength.

She felt a great need well up inside her to take away the anguish she had unintentionally inflicted on him. Knowing that he distrusted relationships meant little to her. It wasn't a relationship she was concerned with at this moment, it was a hurting human being. One that she had grown to care very deeply for.

As she touched his lips with hers, the flashlight flickered out.

9

WHEN RULE REALIZED what was happening, he jerked back, surprised. "What in hell . . . ?"

His shocked remark sobered her, and she sat back. "I—I just wanted to make you feel better."

"I don't want your pity."

"It's not pity," she denied. "I—I care about you, Rule. I guess I didn't learn much from your warning this afternoon."

He muttered a curse. "I was an ass this afternoon." She felt his hands slide up her arms to her elbows. "I've been trying to find a way to apologize all evening. That's why I followed you out to the beach." His breath ruffled her hair pleasantly in the darkness. She inhaled, enjoying the vague hint of coffee.

"It's not necessary. I shouldn't have kissed you. It was foolish." Her heart fluttered as his thumbs moved seductively along the sensitive inner side of her arms.

"We both went a little crazy, I guess." He chuckled without mirth. "The Danforth curse must be catching."

She swallowed, offering dully, "My—er the flashlight went out."

"That's not exactly a news flash."

"What do we do now?"

"I'd say looking for the treasure is out. What would a Bluebird do?"

She smiled wanly, knowing he couldn't see her doing it. What would he think if she said she'd like to stay here with him in the darkness, listening to his voice reverberate in the narrow passage? To have him take her gently in his arms, to lie back and hold her, kiss her, make love to her? She mentally shook herself. Dangerous thinking!

With her mind still lingering on how nice his hands felt on her arms, she ventured with true brilliance, "We'll have to feel our way." She squeezed her eyes shut and hoped Rule wouldn't catch the remark for the Freudian slip that it was.

She sensed rather than saw his head incline toward her. "My thinking exactly," he drawled softly. He'd caught the slip.

This time it was her turn to move away, before she did something crazy again. Her body moved reluctantly, unwilling to break contact with him. She grew frustrated with herself. She was going to have to have a serious chat with her libido.

She had no business kissing this man. After all, wasn't she leaving soon to take up her career, and hadn't Rule already said he was leery of relationships? With false brightness, she suggested, "We'd better get started."

She began to pull up on her knees, but found resistance in his hold on her arms. His mouth touched hers lightly, a mere taste. The electricity in the soft touch seared her to her core, weakening her legs and her resolve. She groaned, whispering, "Rule, this afternoon you said—"

"Damn this afternoon," he muttered, his lips nipping hers. His tongue slid along the contours of her stiffened mouth. "I love the way you smell, Mandy, the fire in you. To hell with everything I said! Use me. . . ."

His hands slid to cradle her body. She heard the moan echo around her before she realized it had come from deep in her own throat. Her nipples went taut, her body turned to mush. It was happening again. She was leaving behind her good sense and becoming something, someone, she didn't know within Rule's embrace.

"We mustn't do this," she whispered desperately, but she clung to him, her fingers fumbling with his shirt-front. "We'll both feel terrible tomorrow."

"Mm-hmm," he murmured in agreement, his lips coming down fully on hers.

Could there be intoxicating fumes in the cave's air, she wondered? She was certainly suffering from something potent and mind-altering. She groaned again, but this time it was a sound of reluctant pleasure. Rule's mouth was open, warm and wet. She could feel his heart thudding against her palms and wanted only to put her face against the furred softness there, to nuzzle and tease the hard, hot flesh until he cried out.

Why did it happen so quickly with this man? By what mystical spell did he make her become such a witch in his arms? A throaty sigh escaped her lips. She opened her mouth wider, responding instinctively to his tongue, nibbling teeth, the velvet, languid heat of his hands as they slid her blouse and bra away.

His mouth moved down, and she quivered with delight as he sampled her neck. She'd always had a sensitive neck, but she had the feeling Rule could bring tree bark to the brink of ecstasy if he were ever so inclined. Her lips trembled with pleasure and she exhaled audibly. Rocking her head against his shoulder, she said, "You must think I'm a nymphomaniac. I can't seem to be alone with you without—" His lips had slid down to nuzzle a breast and Mandy's words caught in her throat.

"All I think is that we've been wasting a lot of energy fighting our need to be lovers," he rasped, his words urgent as he drew her into his mouth, sucking tenderly.

When his words soaked in, her throat closed. Lovers? What graphic reality that thought presented to her. Lovers. To Mandy, though she had never had a lover— except as a husband first—she had great respect for what the word meant. It was more than mere sex to her. It meant trusting, and commitment, a total sharing of two lives. An odd fear swelled within her, dousing her desire. With trembling limbs, she pushed him away. She surprised herself with a low, guttural moan as his tantalizing mouth released her throbbing nipple.

"What is it, darling?" he murmured, his voice tinged with doubt.

"Rule . . . we can't . . ." She felt him pulling her close, felt the soft curls of his hair graze her shoulder as he buried his face between her breasts, kissing her in the delicate hollow there. She caught her trembling lower lip with her teeth. On their own, her arms wound around his head. "Oh, Rule..." she sobbed, kissing the top of his head, her tears dampening the musky curls. "We can't be lovers. You don't even trust me to be with your little girl. Somebody could find the treasure tomorrow, and you'd be gone. And there's Peter..."

With an effort that exhausted her both in body and soul, she pressed against his shoulders, pushing his warmth away. In a broken voice, she whispered, "There are too many problems we'd have to work out first. And you as much as said you don't trust relationships. How can we be lovers?"

His broad, strong arms lingered around her, a painful reminder of the gentle ecstasy she was throwing away. She could hear him breathing, could feel the heated weight of it tickle and tease her naked breasts as he labored to restore his composure. She dared not even try to imagine his face. Probably angry, definitely frustrated. Closing her eyes, she squeezed desperate tears down her cheeks. "You understand, don't you, Rule?"

It took a long time for him to answer. In utter silence he sat there, so near, his warmth, his scent surrounding her with intimate, sensuous messages she fought hard to deny.

Finally, she felt his arms leave her, but before he let go completely, he grasped the narrow ridge of her shoulders, his voice low and tense. "Understand? Hell, I'd rather have you make love to me and scream out Peter's name. I didn't know how good I had it." He let his hands drop, mumbling to himself, "I should have kept my mouth shut."

She winced at the pain in his voice. "I'm glad you didn't. I haven't been thinking. With you it's hard for me to think . . . clearly."

"Hell, I'm not recruiting you for a debating team. I just want to make love to you, for as long as we're able. Someday you're going to have to let Peter go. And my daughter has nothing to do with you and me. You're making something complicated that's really very simple. I just want to love you."

"You mean you want to have sex with me."

"Damn! I can't believe I'm sitting in a cave with a half-naked woman arguing terminology. This is a first for me."

"You're angry."

"Me? Angry?" he refuted, his voice tightly controlled. "I'm too bent over with lust to be angry. Give me a minute."

She couldn't help a tremulous smile. How many men could be rejected this far into the act of making love and come out half this gallant? She had to give him credit for that. In an effort to lighten the situation, she teased kindly, "You must be a pathetic sight, all bent over like that."

"You're a real ego builder, you know." She felt something nudge her arm. "Here. Put on your clothes before I change my mind and ravage you under this romantic canopy of napping bats."

She struggled into the frilly undergarment. "You wouldn't do that. You're a decent man."

His exhale was long and low. "That'll look fine on my tombstone. You dressed?"

"Yes," she said, standing up. "If you'll move off the quilt I can gather it up."

"I'll do it."

"Where's your hat?" she asked suddenly.

"Forget the damned hat."

"Oh, dear," Mandy moaned. "I just realized . . ."

"What now?" He sounded leery.

"Guano deposits. I'm not wearing any shoes."

"Shit," he muttered under his breath.

She winced at the irritation in his voice. "That's another way of putting it, I guess."

"Here, take these." He pressed the quilt and dead flashlight at her. Before she could question him about his plans, he'd swept her up in his arms. She squealed, but in her breathless surprise, she made no sound. "What are you doing?" she asked, fumbling to grab his neck.

"I have on boots."

"Rule—er—besides the guano, be careful of holes. Some are quite deep."

"Check," he grumbled sardonically. "Anything else I should know?"

"Nothing I can think of."

"Good," he grunted, shifting her to a better position. "I was beginning to have nasty doubts about Bluebird preparedness." He took a step. "Oh, hell!"

"What's wrong?"

"I found my hat," he groused.

"I'm sorry."

"That makes two of us."

As he felt his way along the edge of the cave, Mandy worked at making conversation to distract him. She ventured, "Peter told me that when he was a boy, he'd tie a string to a rock and drop it down these holes. The string was fifty feet long. Some places he never hit bottom." She hurried on, explaining, "I know I'm rambling, but I want you to know the man that Peter was as I knew him—a nice, quiet guy, a loner because of a lonely childhood. I don't want you to think of him as a ghostly lover or some kind of rival." She wished she could see Rule's face, judge his reaction, but since she couldn't, and since he wasn't responding, she decided just to keep talking. "Peter loved this cave. He told me he used to collect pieces of crystal deposits from in here—pretended they were millions and millions of dollars—"

"Did Peter make love to you in this cave?" Rule cut in.

"Why. . . of course not."

"Good. I wouldn't care to hear about it if he had. Mind if we don't talk about Peter?"

"Sorry. . ." That had been stupid. Obviously discussing Peter with Rule would never be a particularly welcome topic. With thinned lips, Mandy rode within the strength of his arms for several minutes feeling a very guilty pleasure at his closeness, a pleasure she knew she shouldn't be feeling. Then an important thought struck. She asked, "You can swim, can't you?"

"Yes, ma'am, and if you don't want me to topple into one of your bottomless pits and prove it, don't wriggle."

"I'm not wriggling," she insisted, knowing that was a bald-faced lie. Being in Rule's arms was not exactly a calming affair. Affair! Poor word choice. "Don't worry, Rule." She patted his shoulder. "We'll find that treasure yet."

"Is that your guts talking again?" He sounded a little winded.

"My guts are very reliable."

"They also weigh a ton."

She poked him in the chest. "You're no gentleman."

"Now you tell me."

His vaguely wistful tone melted her heart. She reached up and touched his cheek. "You don't fool me with this gruff act. You're a good guy, Rule Danforth. Even if we can't be lovers, I'm glad we're friends."

She could feel the muscles clench and bunch in his jaw. When she glanced up she was surprised to see him looking down at her from behind narrowed eyes. He looked annoyed. She couldn't really blame him.

He *looked* annoyed? She spun around almost upending them both. "Rule!"

He grunted, grabbing her more firmly to him. "What is it, now?"

"There's the entrance. Can you see it?" She pointed toward the faint, jagged outline of the cave opening. Hugging him with relief, she breathed, "We're saved."

"Hallelujah," he mumbled cynically.

THE NEXT MORNING had been tough for both of them, and it hadn't been because the day had dawned under a blanket of fog. They interacted in a polite verbal dance, talking but not really talking. Like the foul weather, a wariness swirled between them, a thick vapor of uncertainty. After an hour of fruitless, uncomfortable searching in the heavy mist, they gave up and went inside.

Mandy was less sure of herself searching the mansion, not as familiar with the layout inside as out. But because she and Rule were still both chafing from last night in the cave, being in close quarters with the other heirs had helped to lessen the strain.

Because today's clue had been 'Down, down, down,' everyone was scurrying around on the main floor because there was no basement in Heath House. Without much inspiration to guide them, Mandy and Rule had decided to investigate the unoccupied wing of the mansion. They'd been working for an hour without success or conversation.

Mandy knew she'd been right to call a halt to their lovemaking last night. She'd made one mistake with Rule, yes. That made her human. To give in again would make her a fool. Even knowing she was right gave her no peace. A nagging little voice kept needling her, telling her that she'd given up quite a bit by placing so many restrictions on what she felt lovers should be.

Why couldn't they just make love—for as long as they were able, as Rule had said? Her little voice had plagued her with that question countless times during the night. Yet every time she was about to weaken, to decide his way was right, she'd come back to the same damning conclusion. In the long run they'd have more sadness than satisfaction from such a shallow, self-serving relationship.

They'd use each other for a time, until one or both of them tired of the game and walked away. She also knew instinctively that if she ever gave herself totally to Rule, she'd have a hard time watching him go. And he would, one day. He'd as much as said so last night.

She sighed, carefully replacing an eighteenth-century Japanese procelain bowl on a dusty Louis XV commode. She stifled a sneeze. The storage room she and Rule were searching hadn't seen a dust mop for a very long time.

The electricity had been turned off in this wing for years. Though the light from the kerosene lantern was meager, she bent to examine a number of framed paintings that were leaning against a wall. As she thumbed through them listlessly, her mind returned to Rule. He hadn't been short with her this morning or acted in any way irritated. Several times she'd caught him looking at her, his gaze soft yet reluctant to linger.

She was startled from her mental wanderings when she noticed that one of the paintings was signed, Toulouse-Lautrec. She shook her head at the very idea that anyone, even an eccentric like Lydia, would have such a valuable piece of artwork stacked in a dark storage room. She stared down at the portrait. It was of a young man with sad, brown eyes. His expression had the same melancholy reluctance as Rule's had shown all morning.

She pulled her upper lip between her teeth, weary of her mind's constant backtracking to a subject that was closed! She and Rule were partners. Business partners. She was sure it was better this way, for both of them. But somehow the word *partners* had a terribly sterile sound now.

"Mandy." Rule touched her arm. "Where did you go? Didn't you hear me?" Though his remark had been quietly spoken, it seemed to ring from the rafters. She jerked her head up feeling as if she'd been caught doing something wrong. The instant his gaze fastened with hers, all her senses became completely involved with him. In the warm flicker of the kerosene lantern his eyes gleamed golden. His scent beckoned. She had trouble finding her voice. "I'm—I'm sorry. What were you saying?"

"I said this morning at breakfast Maybelle told us what they intended to do with the fortune if they found it."

"Oh." Mandy was curious. "What? Invest in forks?"

He smiled, a slight crook at the corner of his mouth. As small as it was, it affected Mandy more than she wanted it to. "Maybe that, too," he said. "But Maybelle told us they want to build a home for retired circus people."

She thought about that, then said, "If there are many like Skizzo the Great, a place to house them seems almost a necessity."

"You may be right."

She lifted the painting for him to see. "If this is any example of Lydia's fortune, the Poppys could make a pretty fair start on building the home with what they'd get by selling this painting alone. I'm no art expert, but I'd guess there's over a million dollars worth of valuables in here collecting dust."

She stood up, and they both scanned the room silently. It was large, filled with furniture, bric-a-brac and paintings, the sight of which would make even the most snobbish antique dealer drool with greed.

Rule inclined his head toward a strange-looking protrusion in one corner of the room. It was built of wood and bowed out in a half circle that extended down from the ceiling to just five feet above the floor. The overhanging structure of wood was heavily carved and painted a muted green. Running in a row across the front, near the bottom, was a band of carved, gilded, medieval shields, each about two feet square. Below the curved portion, against either wall, two rough stone columns supported the structure.

When they got closer, Mandy said, "Why, it's a fireplace." She ran a hand over a carved cluster of grapes that adorned the shield on the far right. "Now I remember. Lydia once said this room was decorated like a medieval-style bar, but since Arnold wasn't a drinker, they closed it off and used it for storage."

Rule was fingering the carved shields, scrutinizing the center one thoughtfully. It held a rather frightening carving of an attacking hound. The animal's expression was fierce, its teeth bared, as it stared with one golden eye.

"Hmm." He turned to look at Mandy. "I think your guts are rubbing off on me."

She grimaced. "That sounds terrible. What are you talking about?"

He indicated the crest. "That's some eye, don't you think?"

"A one-eyed dog? It's repulsive, if that's what you mean."

"I have a feeling it's more than what it appears to be." He pressed his thumb into the eye's center. An instant later, a loud rumbling invaded the quiet, then a scraping sound, as the room trembled around them. With a gasp, Mandy jumped back, shocked to see the block walls behind the fireplace slowly grind apart to reveal a narrow passageway. It led down steep steps into total darkness.

Mandy looked at Rule, her eyes wide. "I don't believe this. How did you do that?"

He caught her gaze and held it without relenting. "I have a way with animals." Though a smile curved his lips, it didn't quite reach his eyes.

That steady gaze, that small smile, spoke more eloquently than any words about what they'd both avoided speaking of all morning. Her rejection.

Or did it? Could it be just the turmoil of her emotions making her read things into his innocent remarks?

Looking away to regain her sense of proportion, she mumbled, "I'll get the lantern."

She'd just picked it up when the door to the storage room flew open and practically everyone in the house crowded in, all shouting questions.

Maybelle shrieked, "What are you two doing in here—bulldozing the place down? Mr. Perth will hear of this. If I can't use the pickax, you can't—"

"Oh, shut up, Maybelle," Steppy snapped. "Can't you see they don't have any heavy equipment in here? You're the only one who came prepared to detonate the island."

"Who rattled your cage, nephew?" Maybelle stalked from the clutter of people, planting herself between Rule and Mandy. "So what's going on, then? What have you done? The whole house was shaking a minute ago."

Rule motioned toward the fireplace. "We were just about to take a walk."

When Maybelle saw the opening behind the fireplace her eyes narrowed in cunning calculation. She whirled toward Mandy, snatching the lantern from her. "Don't you have some gardening to do?" she queried archly.

"No, I—my job is done," Mandy stammered, surprised to be singled out for Maybelle's venomous attention.

"She's helping me," Rule explained.

Turning a sharp glare on him, Maybelle spat, "She's using you, you mean!" With a caustic laugh, she added,

"Like they say, there's one born every minute. I hope you're getting something for all her so-called help."

Rule gave a small grimace that could have been construed as regret or resignation before his expression hardened. "Say what you want about me, Maybelle. We Danforths have never been noted for our sound thinking. But you owe Mrs. McRae an apology."

"Why, you young Jack-a-dandy!" Maybelle screeched. "Who do you think you are?"

Though she tried, Mandy couldn't detach her uneasy gaze from Rule's somber profile as he stared at his aunt in silent warning.

"I think you'd better go with the apology idea, Aunt Maybelle," Steppy chided. "My suggestion is much messier."

Rule half grinned at his cousin before looking at Mandy. "The remark was unforgivable. I hope you'll consider the source and be able to forget it."

"Don't you *dare* apologize for me! I can do my own apologizing—"

"Good," Rule broke in. "That's what I wanted to hear."

Mandy blushed at the unwanted attention but said nothing.

Maybelle was obviously put out at being so easily thwarted. Stomping over the hearth and crouching to duck beneath the carved overhang, she headed into the dark passage. "Coming Skizzo?"

With a high-pitched giggle, Henry dislodged himself from the crowd of servants and heirs hovering at the door. Rule turned to Mandy, catching her with his penetrating gaze. "That remark was crude, even for her. I'm really sorry."

"It wasn't your fault, Rule." With a small smile in repayment for his gallant defense, she added, "Don't worry about it."

Without further words, he took her elbow and led her into the fireplace behind Maybelle. Scurrying little footsteps told Mandy that Henry was not far behind.

"Well, hell's bells," Steppy spat. "Come on, Savina. We're entitled to see this, too."

"Don't push me, Danforth!" Maybelle shouted over her shoulder.

"I think Henry's behind you," Rule returned after his uncle had scurried by him and scampered after Maybelle, who was taking the steps two at a time.

"Be careful," Rule called. "These steps are steep."

Maybelle cackled. "A lot you care."

Rule and Mandy exchanged glances. The light was dim, but Mandy could see frustration glinting in his eyes.

Trying to lighten his mood, she whispered, "Your aunt should open a charm school."

"Right."

She smiled wryly, but said nothing else. The light was too dim and the steps too steep for them to concentrate on anything other than staying upright. The staircase creaked and moaned under the sudden barrage of foot traffic. Some of the steps were so badly warped that Mandy needed all her concentration to keep her footing. Once they reached the bottom, it was clear that they were in an underground cavern.

"This must be part of the cave," Mandy whispered to Rule. "It narrows down to an opening too small to follow a little beyond where we were last night...." She winced when he squinted at the reminder. Hurriedly, she went on. "I had no idea the cavern got wide again."

"What's all this stuff?" Steppy huffed as he and Savina entered. They'd all raised dust from the dirt floor, and Savina waved at the thick air, coughing.

. "Barrels—" She sneezed. "Big metal containers, piles of dusty bottles."

"I think the welded oval containers are copper, but the years have turned them black," Steppy observed.

"Looks like a place where bootleg whisky was manufactured," Rule suggested. "Is that possible, Savina?"

Apparently Savina had not expected Rule to address her directly. She glanced over at him and then looked quickly away. "Well," she began hesitantly. "Lydia did say her daddy was a wild sort, made lots of money illegally before he got sent up for income tax evasion. This could be what she meant."

"*Could* be," Steppy laughed. "I'd say it could be. Looks like Lydia had plenty of money of her own—ill-gotten though it was. I thought she married old Arnold for his money." He turned to Rule, shrugging apologetically. "Sorry, old man. But that's the rumor."

"Don't mind me." Rule smiled crookedly. "I hear it's done all the time."

"Oh, it's true. Lydia said she was broke when she married Arnold," Savina explained. "She told me she went out and stalked rich men just like they were big jungle cats. She needed one wealthy enough to save Barren Heath Isle from being sold for back taxes. She thought Arnold was cute and kind of naive, so she decided on him." This time she turned directly to face Rule before she went on. "She also said that a couple of years after they were married, she really did fall in love with him. Interesting how things turn out. You go after a guy for what you can get, then..." She shrugged and turned away, entangling her gaze with Steppy's. "Well, you never know," she finished softly. From where Mandy was standing, she could still see Savina's eyes. There was something odd in the look, not mean or calculating, but almost tender.

Did Savina DeWitt, the conniving little yuppie, really care about poor insecure Steppy Wrathmore? That would be an ironic twist if it were true. She shook off the thought. She didn't have time to puzzle over that now. "Maybe we ought to get organized," she said. "I'll go back up and get flashlights. Rule, you divide us up so that each couple searches different areas—"

"Why Rule?" barked Maybelle. "I was first down here. I'll decide who looks where."

Savina shouted, "You old biddy! Just keep your mean mouth shut for a change. Steppy and I'll search the shelves on the far side. Rule and Mandy can search the copper things and you and your little...little forker can go stuff yourselves in a barrel for all I care. How's that for a plan!"

"Why you . . . you—"

"Come on, Steppy." Savina took his hand and tugged him away. "We don't have to listen to her."

"Are you going to let that little gold digger talk to your aunt and uncle that way?" she bellowed at Rule.

His eyes flicked from Savina's retreating form to his aunt. With a casual shrug, he remarked, "Women's lib is a fact, Maybelle. I can't tell any woman how to act. Not even you—no matter how much you may need it."

Maybelle snorted her disgust. "Come, Henry." She grabbed him by the lapel and dragged him toward a stack of barrels, snarling, "That young pup just tried to insult me."

"Never mind, my little peach pit," he soothed as he stumbled along in her wake. "I don't think he tried very hard."

"My, my..." Jetta stepped out of the darkness that housed the staircase. "This place is a brilliant find. Perfect for today's clue." Her laughter flowed like warm honey in the stagnant chamber. "You can't get much more 'down' than this."

Mandy nudged Rule's arm. "I'll run up and get the flashlights."

"Maybe your guts weren't so far wrong last night," Rule remarked quietly to Mandy, his voice only vaguely grim.

Jetta caught his words and asked, "What happened last night?"

Mandy's face heated. Excusing herself, she hurried to the staircase. After she'd mounted a few steps and was out of sight, she stopped, flattening herself against the wall. Her heart pounded so loudly that she had the unreasonable fear that it would echo throughout the cavern for everyone to hear. She strained to catch Rule's answer. She knew he wouldn't tell Jetta what had actually happened between them in the cave, but for some demented reason she had to know what he would say.

"We searched the cave," Rule explained minimally.

"At night?" Jetta asked, incredulous. "That place is bad enough in the daylight. It must be hell in the dark."

"Close enough." His voice sounded empty, leeched of emotion.

Mandy closed her eyes and tipped her head back tiredly. She knew what he meant.

10

JETTA ENFOLDED Rule's arm in hers and swept him toward the light that Maybelle had set on an upright barrel. She whispered conspiratorially, "You have a way about you, cousin. I could go for you." She winked. "But since we're related, any kids we'd have would probably be a little strange."

He laughed. "Considering our heritage so far, I think they'd be more than a little strange."

She smiled, her even teeth shining in the semidarkness. "I suppose we must think of the future sanity of the world." She tweaked him on the chin. "While we're on the subject of love, have you noticed a chubby, winged fellow called Cupid rearing his ugly little head on this island?"

He looked at her, lifting a skeptical brow. He felt a vague unease, as though his privacy were about to be invaded. He hedged, "Never heard of the guy."

"Oh?" She sounded amused. "How'd you get that little girl of yours? Parcel post?"

"Okay," he conceded. "Maybe Cupid screwed up a long time ago. The only redeeming part of that ordeal was Dana. Since then, I've become one helluva great arrow dodger. You can forget the subtle prying, because I'm not in love with anybody."

Her eyes had widened at the steely edge in his tone. But a fraction of a second later they were flickering with a mild humor that bothered him. "I hadn't planned on prying, Rule," she purred. "I was talking about Steppy and Savina. Why did you think I was talking about you?"

An odd mixture of annoyance and relief rushed over him. Before he could form an answer, her laughter filled the room. "Never mind. You've said enough."

He hadn't said anything, dammit! He hadn't even thought anything. He scowled, wondering what she found so funny.

"Who's that? Jetta?" Maybelle turned around, squinting. "Oh, good. Run upstairs and get my pickax. It's in the grand ballroom."

Jetta's smile faded and she muttered, "And I know just where I'd like to put your pickax, you old—"

"What did you say?" Maybelle called, her head disappearing into a barrel.

Irritated now, Jetta yelled back, "*Never mind.* Grand ballroom? Why not? Where else would my mother's pickax be?" As she pivoted to leave, she passed Rule a smirk. "Oh, by the way, give Mandy my regards."

Her words halted him in midstride, and he frowned at nothing in particular. Mandy? Was Jetta suggesting that he was in love with Mandy? His gaze roved the darkness restlessly. He was not pleased with the idea. Still, it wasn't as though the same thing hadn't occurred to him. Not exactly love, maybe, but close enough to be bothersome at three o'clock in the morning when he got the sweats just recalling her face, or the way her cheeks flushed when she was embarrassed. Hell! Even the way she held her violin, her face all pinched with concentration, was ridiculously endearing.

Around dawn, he'd finally convinced himself that Mandy was a fine, sensible woman with high morals, and he'd been a bum for trying to turn her into any-

thing less. He hadn't intended to think about it anymore.

He recalled how devastated he'd felt when she'd
turned him down last night. The memory made his
belly knot up and a fire begin to burn in his gut. It
wasn't just a pleasant round of sex he'd lost. Though
she'd been right about that, at least in part. He sure as
hell did want to have sex with her. Sex with Mandy was
something he didn't like to believe he'd never experience again. He wanted to take her to bed, and he
wanted it very badly.

But that wasn't all. It wasn't purely physical this time,
as it had been with previous women. There were little
things about Mandy, things she did, ways she had of
looking at him that made him feel clean and warm—
like the desert on mornings after a rare summer rain.
He wanted more than a physical relationship with her.
He wanted permanence.

He closed his eyes. Where the hell had that come
from? His plans didn't include getting involved. Not
anymore. Caring about another person brought nothing but hell with it.

Jamming his hands in his pockets, he headed toward
darkness, not caring what he ran into. Maybe what he
needed was a good bash in the head to clear his mind.

"I've got them," Mandy called, her voice breathless,
echoing in the low-ceilinged chamber. "All I could find."

He half turned, his gaze straying reflexively to her.
She was walking toward him, her arms loaded with
flashlights. She had been right, of course. He'd known
it all night long, with every curse and every tick of the
clock. It would be wrong for them to become lovers.
She was too sensitive, and she'd end up being hurt. He
didn't want to hurt her.

As he watched her coming slowly toward him, he wondered if she had any idea how incredibly lovely she was. He studied her for a moment from beneath lowered lids, then dropped his gaze to the dirt at his feet. She wouldn't be the only one who'd get hurt, he admitted grudgingly. He was in enough pain as it was.

"Rule," Mandy called again, sounding doubtful. "Didn't you hear me?"

He faced her then, knowing a longing that was very close to debilitating. "Sorry, I must have been thinking about something else." He extended a hand. "Pitch me one."

LUNCH CAME and went. By four o'clock, they were all filthy and exhausted. Mandy sank to the floor, leaning wearily against the rough cave wall. "Any other idea?" she asked Rule as he scanned the pitted walls with his flashlight for the hundredth time.

"To be honest, I don't think Lydia even knew about this place. She couldn't have been much more than a child when prohibition was repealed. I'd guess it's been half a century since a human being's been down here."

"I have a feeling you're right—"

"I still think we ought to have a go at that entrance that's sealed off with cement blocks," Maybelle interrupted, joining them.

"Go ahead," Rule said. "But those bricks are black with mildew. They haven't been disturbed in years."

"Besides, Mrs. Poppy," Mandy added, "the only reason for blocking that cave entrance off was probably to keep out water that would have rushed down during big storms and ruined their distilling equipment. The cave gets so small on the other side that you'd have to crawl to get in that way, maybe not even then. I think it'd be a waste of your time."

Maybelle passed a glare from one to the other, then nodded curtly. "Well, maybe it can wait." Wheeling away, she left them alone.

Rule and Mandy glanced at each other, surprised by her easy acquiescence. Rule cocked his head toward the stairs. "Jetta, Steppy and Savina have given up here. Ready to try someplace else?"

Mandy nodded. "After a bath."

Rule took her arm and helped her up. "Where do you suggest we look with a clue like 'Down, down, down'?"

She wiped her hand across her face to clear her eyes of stray wisps of hair. "The *Titanic*?" She sighed with fatigue.

He laughed. He didn't analyze the reason. All he knew was for the first time today the mood was genuine.

"I didn't think it was that funny," Mandy remarked, her expression quizzical. "You must be tired."

"Maybe." His eyes roamed tenderly over her. She was so tempting, all smudged and dishevelled. Only half kidding, he said, "Let's go take a shower."

She raised her dirty chin, meeting his gaze. He grinned. There was something both shy and sensuous about those parted lips that made Mandy feel weak. With an effort to keep her voice normal, she quipped, "Let's take two, and call each other in the morning."

"I thought I was the doctor," he said, his steady look making her heart pound quickly.

Dropping her gaze, she countered in a low whisper, "But I'm no wild ass."

"You can't prove that by me," he assured her. The sensuous undertone of his voice caused an unwanted quiver along her spine. Her heartbeats suddenly coming uneven and hard, she turned a stony glare on him. No words were needed to get her message across.

"I'll make mine a cold shower," Rule muttered.

Her eyes stung and she realized with self-disgust that she was on the verge of tears. She was trying to do the right thing here. Why couldn't he, damn him? With a swipe at her eyes, she hurried away from him toward the stairs.

"Where do we meet?" he called after her. "The meadow?"

"In an hour," she managed in a weak but miraculously steady voice before she mounted the steps and rushed away. Her shower, too, she decided with regret, would be cold.

MANDY PUT her hands to her cheeks; they were flaming. She'd known they would be. She'd been so embarrassed. The icy water had hit her skin in the shower, and she'd shrieked so loud that Papa Josh had limped to the door and pounded, worried that she'd fallen and hurt herself. She'd been hard pressed to explain why she was bathing in ice water.

She'd also been hard pressed to explain why she'd decided to wear her favorite white blouse and pink drop-waist jumper. She didn't want to admit, even to herself, that she wanted to look pretty and feminine for Rule. After all, she'd made a little speech last night that made a lot of sense, about how and why they couldn't be lovers. So why did she want Rule to admire the way she looked? It was inconsistent with logic. Wouldn't that just add fuel to the fire that never quite went out between them?

She touched her hair. It was still slightly wet. She'd left it unbraided and tied it at her neck with a pink ribbon. The sandy curls danced in the breeze as they dried. She wondered if Rule would notice. She had mixed feelings about what she wanted from him. She hoped to heaven she wasn't using him, as he'd suggested. But even though she struggled to keep alive her precious memories of Peter, she had also been struggling with her more recent, terribly potent memories of Rule. His taste, his scent, all stimulated her beyond her ability to resist him. She'd never known such wild elation in a man's arms before, even when Peter had made love to her.

Could it be remotely possible that she was just voraciously hungry for the caress of a man after all the time alone? She lifted her eyes to the overcast sky, unable to answer with total assurance. She'd just never felt this way about anyone before—helplessly and insatiably drawn. All she knew for sure was that the idea of seeing Rule walk out of her life grew more objectionable with each day they spent together.

"Hi." Rule's voice was so close that it startled her. She stopped short. When she turned to greet him, her skirt lapped ahead of her, stroking and patting his jeans. Feeling an odd sense of guilt that the contact had somehow been her doing instead of the impetuous breeze, she took a step away from him.

"Oh, hello." She smiled shyly, brushing curls from her eyes. "I didn't see you there."

"I know," he drawled, his eyes taking a slow, easy trip from her head to her toes. "You were frowning so deeply in thought that you didn't hear me the first three times I spoke. Something wrong?"

"No." She shook her head, hoping her denial looked absolute. "Oh, by the way, I mixed up too much tuna salad for just Josh and me. I—er—Josh wanted me to invite you to eat with us, if you'd like."

His eyes lifted to her face, a hint of surprise in them. "Thanks." He smiled. "I'm getting a little tired of eating in the mansion. It's like sharing a meal with a pack of rabid dogs."

"Any good food fights yet?" she asked, trying the keep the conversation superficial.

"I expect to get a mousse in the face any day now." He put a hand on her elbow, taking her off guard. "Where do you suggest we search? We'll be losing light in an hour or so."

"I was thinking maybe the beach on the far side of the island. It's the lowest place. Pretty flat and not many places to hide anything. But . . ." She lifted a shoulder in a shrug.

"I know. However else I feel about Lydia, we have to give her credit. She's hidden her fortune very well. It's getting to the point where one place seems about as good as the next."

Mandy nodded but said nothing more. They walked in silence for a long time, with Rule gently helping her over fallen logs or snarls of shrubbery. When at last they were almost to the beach, Rule's pull on her arm halted her. She turned to look up at him, but when she saw his finger held to his lips, she didn't speak. He indicated the beach. Not far away, Mandy could see Steppy, half hidden by a pile of boulders. His camera was poised at his eye. He snapped, held it away from his face and smiled down at something hidden from their view.

"Savi, honey, I wish you'd take them off, really. It'd be so much more natural."

"Oh, Steppy, I just couldn't," she objected in a sweet pout. "I'd feel naked."

Rule and Mandy exchanged glances. Rule's was amused, Mandy's shocked.

"Come on, Savi, they're only eyelashes. And your hair, you wear it too severely. If you'd take out the pins and muss it with your fingers, you'd look gorgeous. Think about Mandy. She's got a real natural beauty about her and she never wears makeup."

Mandy blushed as Savina retorted, "Mandy's okay, I guess, for an older woman."

Rule's chuckle forced Mandy's eyes up to meet his. They were twinkling merrily. He winked at her. It was a very sensual act when performed by those gold-flecked eyes.

"Come on," Steppy was coaxing, "take them off and let down your hair. I'll develop the pictures tonight and you'll see I'm right. You're a beautiful woman, Savina. You trust my judgment, don't you?"

"You know I do, Steppy." There was a pause. "Okay," she said reluctantly. "But only for you."

Rule bent near Mandy's ear. "Maybe we'd better leave those two alone."

Mandy agreed with a small nod. They circled back, away from the beach, not speaking until they were well out of earshot. Then Rule remarked, "I thought she was just using him to get in on the fortune. But I don't know anymore. Jetta thinks they're falling in love."

Mandy looked over her shoulder. The beach was hidden by an outcropping of pines. "I think it's sweet—those two yuppies finding each other. I'd never have picked them as a loving couple."

"I don't think Savina would have, either, at first."

"Emma told me once that Savina sleeps in those lashes, just in case the mansion burns down. If Steppy could get her to take them off, then it's definitely love."

"Somehow, between the two of them, they're growing up," Rule observed mildly.

"That's what love is all about—becoming something better with someone else."

Her gave her a lingering look. His eyes were tender. "You know, you look too fetching to be so wise."

Her heart leaped against her ribs. How silly to feel jubilant just because a man gave her a small compliment. But it hadn't been just any man. After all, Steppy had said she was beautiful, but it had been Rule's wink that had buoyed her spirits. She glanced uncertainly around, at a loss for words.

"There I go again," he muttered. "I guess that cold shower's worn off."

"Mine too—" She cut herself off as soon as she realized what she'd said, but it hadn't been soon enough. She squeezed her eyes shut, horrified. It was one thing to inwardly, secretly enjoy his compliments, it was another thing entirely to let him know how forcefully he affected her.

"What?" His question was light with laughter.

She ran a fidgety hand along her nape, quelling a tingle. Eyeing him in the neck, she explained, "The hot water heater is on the blink back at the cottage."

"I see." He nodded sagely, more than a touch of amusement in his tone. "These things happen."

Her gaze drifted on its own up to connect with his eyes. It was a nerve-racking trip over handsome, amused terrain. She stammered, "It—it's a very old hot water heater, and . . ." She opened her mouth and then closed it again several times, trying to go on with the lie, but the laughter in his eyes stymied her. With a stout little "Harumph", she started forward, her back a bit too straight for comfortable walking. "I'm going to search the sex—the suck—er—"

"Works for me," he drawled.

Her face sizzled, "I mean, the *stream!* Under the bridge in the formal garden. You don't have to come."

"Wouldn't miss it." His voice rang with mirth, turning Mandy's insides to fiery pulp. He was certainly enjoying her humiliation. Maybe, in some sick way, he was paying her back for her rejection of him last night. If that was his plan, it was working.

SEVERAL DISMAL, rainy days trudged by, throwing the company on Barren Heath Isle well into their third week of searching. Tired, keyed up and irritable, the family members were at one anothers' throats. Jetta had threatened her parents while wielding her mother's whip. Savina and Steppy had begun to avenge themselves for Maybelle's constant belittling. This morning they had nailed her bedroom door shut only to have Maybelle pickax her way out.

Rule's mood had gone from an exhilarating rush, that day when Mandy had admitted to taking a cold shower—well, almost admitted to it—to an uneasy discontent. From that moment near the beach until now, Mandy had kept her distance. She'd made sure that their conversations were business oriented and brief. She'd hardly even exchanged so much as friendly eye contact with him. With Mother Nature throwing in thunderstorms alternating with fog, Rule couldn't figure how things could have gotten much worse—until moments ago.

When he'd heard the bad news, he'd just walked away. At first he'd had no particular destination in mind, but soon it had been obvious even to him where he was heading. The bride's garden. Mandy had mentioned she'd be spending the noon hour there.

The gate swung open with the mandatory creak, announcing his presence. Mandy, who was pruning a bank of silver rose bushes, looked up. There must have been something in his expression that hinted at trouble, because she dropped her aloof facade, her eyes growing wide and concerned. "What is it, Rule?" she asked in a low breath.

He took a step forward, allowing the gate to bang shut at his back. Ignoring her question for the moment, he scanned the distant ocean. It was flat and metal gray, fusing with a leaden sky. Not a pretty day for leaving. With an effort, he turned back. His eyes wandered over her for a moment before he asked, "Why are you out here working, when your job's over?"

She peered at him curiously, obviously wondering what might be wrong. But she didn't ask. Instead she said, "I—I suppose I just can't stand to see the lovely place go to seed."

"I know." He grinned tiredly. "I feel the same way about one particularly lovely widow."

With her searching glance, he went on, "If I'd found the treasure, I'd have been happy to have both you and Josh stay on, Mandy. I just wanted you to know that."

"If?" she repeated in a tight whisper.

He nodded, his eyes grave.

Mandy dropped her shears, just missing her sandaled feet. "*Oh, no!*" she cried, covering her mouth with trembling fingers. "Who?"

"Maybelle," he said. "With her metal detector."

She inhaled shakily and tilted her face up to the darkened sky. "Where?"

"The beach, on the other side of the island. About where we saw Steppy and Savina."

Mandy felt her legs slowly crumble beneath her, and she grasped the fountain's edge. It was over. Everything was over. For her, for Josh, for Rule and his propagation center. She had no idea it would hit her this hard. "Oh, no..." she moaned, leaning heavily against stone. "I can't believe it." Her eyes stung with angry, defeated tears. "It can't be, can't be...."

She felt strong arms coming around her, cradling her, pulling her to rest against a warm, familiar chest, as Rule whispered, "It's hard, I know." His lips grazed her ear, and without care for the right or wrong of it, she nestled nearer, allowing her tears to flow freely.

"Oh, Rule," she whimpered softly. "I wanted this for you—for Josh. I'm so sorry...."

"It wasn't meant to be." His breath feathered her hair, skimmed her cheek. She closed her eyes, sighing brokenly.

"Mandy," he whispered, after a long minute. "I've been thinking a lot about what I'd do if this happened. My next move is to find land somewhere, and soon."

She nodded. "I know. Where do you think you'll go?"

"It doesn't matter. Just somewhere where land is cheap." She felt him shift, turning her around to face him. When she opened her eyes, her gaze tangled with his. "I have no right to say this. I know I'd be asking you to give up a good job." He paused, his eyes searching hers. "I'll have to deal with your feelings about Peter.... But I want you with me."

She stared, unsure she'd heard him right. With a smile of breathtaking sweetness, Rule ran a hand through her hair, murmuring, "I love you." His arms brought her close, and he spoke against her cheek. "Mandy, everything ends. Love...even species. We try to stop it—sometimes we can't. I won't ask you for forever. Just stay with me for as long as you can."

The grave, impassioned words seemed torn from his throat, and Mandy was moved to the marrow of her bones. "Rule," she managed through trembling lips. "Are you asking me to marry you?"

"Marry me, yes. Be my lover.... Whatever you want. I'll take you on whatever terms you say."

Though she opened her lips, she couldn't speak. She was too shocked, to stunned to even think.

Gently he traced lean fingers along her cheek, then lightly kissed the place, still tingling from his touch. When he lifted his face away, his eyes were sad. Plainly able to see her distress, he added gently, "I know you're not ready for a commitment. Hell! I don't have anything to offer you, not even a roof."

Mandy's heart was a painful knot in her chest. In her wildest fantasies she'd never seen this coming. How did she feel about Rule? Was her love for Peter strong enough to sustain her beyond the time Rule was gone? Was her attraction to Rule a result of loneliness, or had she fallen in love with him?

And what of her job? It certainly would be a chance of a lifetime for her. She searched his face. He was watching her, his gaze unwavering, hypnotically sweet. She swallowed hard, finally finding her voice. "This is so—so new, Rule, I—I just can't . . ." Her throat closed.

He reluctantly released her and stood. "I understand." Covering her hand with his, he squeezed just enough to still the trembling of her fingers. "I had to tell you how it is," he whispered hoarsely. "Guess I'll take a walk."

Mandy sat stiffly on the fountain's edge as he went away, unbowed, even in the face of crushing defeat. By the time the gate had clattered shut behind him, her eyes were so misted with unshed tears that he had become nothing more than a proud, lanky blur.

SHE GAZED after him, remembering all over again how handsome he was, how honest and downright nice. . . . She recalled how marvelous his arms had felt around her. And he'd asked her to marry him. Inhaling shakily, she slid off the fountain's edge and groped for her pruning shears. With the back of her hand she swiped at her tears, then whacked away absentmindedly at the rosebush.

Naturally, she couldn't marry him. It was just as he'd said. She wasn't ready for a commitment. She gritted her teeth, pressing hard on the handles to deal with a stubborn branch. When it succumbed and fell away, several silver blossoms tumbled to earth with it.

She was to be a partner in a fancy landscape architectural firm, with very exclusive clients. She could write her own ticket. It was the chance of a lifetime. Another branch hit the mulch with hardly a sound to mark its demise. How many other landscape architects did Mandy know her age who were so fortunate? None. Not one!

She downed another limb, and its collection of virgin buds fell across one foot, unnoticed. Besides, Rule knew she couldn't give up Peter's memory just like that. She'd loved him. He'd been her husband for eight years. Rule couldn't expect her to just ignore all that and run off to some lonely, far-off . . .

Her throat closed with a dawning horror. It wasn't some dusty, nameless Midwestern plain she was picturing in her mind's eye as lonesome and far-off. It was Chicago, a bustling metropolis full of vital people, fascinating places and things. Chicago just lacked one vital element. Rule Danforth.

All at once, the idea of becoming a partner in a high-and-mighty landscape architectural firm seemed a desolate fate. The realization stunned her, and she stared, wide-eyed, at the rosebush for a very long time, hardly breathing.

She was in love with Rule Danforth. She'd never used him, never merely lusted after him out of loneliness or a libido gone berserk. She'd known it all along, she supposed, but she'd fought a hearty fight against admitting it. Even the rosebush before her was a testament to that.

"Oh, you poor mutilated little thing." She laughed sadly, gathering branches choked with blossoms from the ground. Dropping her shears, she clutched the makeshift bouquet to her chest and promised the scrawny bush, "Don't worry. You'll be okay. We both will."

It seemed only seconds later when Mandy found herself standing just beyond the hidden entrance to the secret garden. Her heart pounded deafeningly in her ears, and her legs were the consistency of warm taffy. She could feel her fear and her passion in every fiber of her body. Still clutching the roses, she peeked inside.

Rule was there. She had no idea how she'd known he would be, but she felt a wild elation just knowing he was near. He was standing stock-still in the shaft of midday sunlight, looking almost too perfect to be real. He was deep in thought, and his stance was straight but with a trace of weariness about the shoulders. His arms were crossed before him, his eyes cast downward, masked by dark, curling lashes. His black hair shone almost blue in the sun, and silky curls fell across his forehead, begging to be mussed.

What was he thinking, she mused. He had the weight of quite a few unsolved problems on his broad shoulders. She hoped that what she had to say would solve at least one of those problems and place a smile on his wide, marvelous lips. With a tremulous clearing of her throat, she pushed through the wispy curtain of branches to stand hesitantly in the deep shade.

At the rustling sound of her entrance, Rule looked her way. He stared, unmoving, questioning. Moments passed. His long, lingering gaze made her inexplicably uneasy. Nervously she clutched the roses and swallowed hard.

"What are you doing here?" he asked finally, his voice hoarse.

"I..." She felt light-headed, and her cheeks grew hot. "I—I just wondered if I could take a few rose cuttings, and maybe a packet or two of flower seeds—to help hold down the dust."

Those wonderful lips opened slightly in surprise. "What dust?" he asked, his eyes glimmering with a new emotion. Could it be hope?

Her smile was shy. "The dust from that cheap chunk of land you want to take me off to. I'm afraid I'd have to insist on having flowers."

"You'd have to insist, would you?" His answering smile was touchingly artless.

She nodded.

He inclined his head toward her bouquet. "Are those for me?"

Feeling silly, she looked down at the confused jumble of roses. Why had she lugged them all the way out here? She cast bashful eyes back up to meet his gaze. "I—I'm afraid when I have a hard problem to work out

I prune, or I play the violin. I'm not sure which is more destructive."

Before she'd realized he'd moved he was there, taking the tangle of roses from her stiffened arms, his eyes kindled with golden flames.

"Let me pretend they're for me." He laid the flowers safely aside. When their eyes met again, he was pulling her to him. "The mad pruner of Barren Heath Isle." He grazed the tip of her upturned nose with a gentle kiss. "You'll fit right into the Danforth family."

She wound her arms about his neck, murmuring beneath his lips, "I love you, Rule."

His eyes darkened and took on a romantic gleam. "I hope so, because I couldn't bear to think of living without you."

A little shiver ran up her spine at the sensual promise in those words.

"Can we take Josh?" she asked, almost too quietly to be heard.

"Of course—he's family." Rule tasted her lips.

"You're wonderful," she breathed, thrusting her chin up and opening her mouth. She was thirsting, like a baby bird, for the nourishment only his lips could offer.

He kissed her deeply then, a slow, hot whisper of experience that set a spark alive in her veins. Their tongues slid together and then apart as he teased the recesses of her mouth and teeth in a sultry, intimate dance. She wanted him so badly that she made a small, tender sound in the back of her throat.

He heard it and pulled his face away from hers, staring down at her wordlessly. His eyes were intent, his expression filled with passion, but he waited.

She knew what he needed to hear from her and she smiled, pulling him down into the soft bed of silver leaves. Feeling playful, she pushed him to his back and slid over him. She kissed his aggressive chin and told him, "Peter would be happy for me, Rule. I know that now." She kissed his delectable lower lip. "If you want me to scream out any names from now on, you'll have to settle for your own."

"I will, will I?" he asked, his voice full of suppressed longing. "Well . . . if that's the way it must be. . . ." His smile was soft as he lifted his head to nip at her lips. "I think I can handle that."

His hands moved down her back to cup her hips as a hushed moan of desire gurgled in Mandy's throat. When she turned her head slightly to catch her breath, she inhaled instead the aroma of pine-scented after-shave mixed with his own dusky scent. It was a heady potion. Her sigh was passion drenched as she whispered, "Love me, Rule."

"I do," he whispered. "I will. For as long as you want me."

"I'll want you forever . . ." she assured him, nibbling his ear.

His hands, exploring beneath her skirt, were weaving a delicious lassitude throughout her body. She closed her eyes and clung to him. The time for words had ended. It was time for a much more basic and natural form of communication—one older than any form of spoken language, and one that would outlast the written word. Their clothes disappeared in a writhing ballet, without sound, but with heated gestures fraught with beauty and ritual.

Desire surged through her as Rule's hands roamed and enlivened her most womanly parts. Knowing fingers took possession of her throbbing core, damp with need. She could do little more than press her cheek against his tan, bronzed chest and glory that this man loved her, and that she was the reason for the lusty acceleration of his heartbeat.

His fingers were a loving instrument, stirring her to such impassioned heights that she circled his broad chest with her arms, offering huskily, "Oh, Rule, take me...."

"Not yet," he breathed against her ear, pulling her more possessively to him. "I want this to be a special time for us."

She clutched his massive shoulders, her body so sensitized by his touch that she didn't know if she could bear the pretty pain another second.

"Rule. Oh, my love..." she cried out, at last, spiraling over the edge of passion's sweetest precipice in exquisite, pulsating slow motion.

An intoxicating trail of minutes slid by. Mandy's body quaked and shivered as the multitude of sensations dwindled slowly away. Her body glowed with satisfaction as she snuggled against him.

"You're a devil, you know," she finally whispered, tears of joy sliding down her hot cheeks.

He shifted, nestling her into the crook of his arm. He looked down, pretending innocence, his eyes still clouded with passion. "I thought I was a cowboy."

She grinned mischievously, then nipped at the curling hairs on his chest. "That's right. And I'm still waiting for a ride." She cast him her most seductive look, catching his languid smile.

"My, my, aren't we impatient," he drawled.

With a buoyant giggle, she replied, "My, my, aren't we self-satisfied, all of a sudden. Why so smug?"

He curled both arms tightly around her pulling her on top of him. "Because, my love—" he slashed a devilish grin "—I'm almost positive I heard my name mentioned a few moments ago."

"You did?" she teased, her breasts swelling again with a hot, urgent need for him. "Just what was that name again?"

He chuckled wickedly. They were lying there, thigh upon thigh, and she could feel his hardness tempting, teasing her with purposeful strokes. His erotic massage was so scandalously well aimed that her womanly core began to pulsate with a heavy, aching need for him to come inside her and make them one. "You're very talented," she breathed, her voice too husky to disguise her desire. "What else can you do?"

He lowered his head, nuzzling the aching walls of her breasts, and murmured, "I hope you like surprises."

"Mmmmm," she sighed, as he slid his hands along her thighs, spreading her legs. Then, lifting her with exquisite finesse, he settled her on his readied staff.

She heard her name in his enraptured moan as they came together, and she smiled. There could be no more beautiful sound in God's universe.

His hands lingered on her hips as she began to move above him. His eyes were closed, his lashes resting heavy on tanned cheeks. The wide, strong mouth was opened slightly in sensual invitation. Swooping down, she snatched a kiss, and his eyes flew open.

"I couldn't resist." She grinned, radiantly happy.

He grinned back. Encircling her waist with his hands, he thrust himself into her even more deeply. She gasped, lolling her head on his chest to savor, for the moment, the rush of delight that coursed through her. "I didn't expect that," she moaned in awe.

"I couldn't resist."

"Please—don't even try." She kissed his chest, her tongue darting, licking the furred hardness. "I could eat you up," she fairly growled.

A highly satisfied laugh rumbled next to her ear. "I'll hold you to that. But for now . . ."

His hips began to move beneath her, shattering all other thought. With impassioned skill, he licked the flames of her desire, awakening her to greater erotic heights than she had dreamed possible. They traveled together, mingled in body and spirit, whispering promises to each other, promises that they both knew would be kept—until another heaven and another earth would pass.

MANDY'S BODY was quivering jello. When she couldn't button her blouse, Rule kissed her trembling fingers and swept them away. "Let me, darling. At this rate we'll be here forever."

She sat back, relishing the warmth of his hands. "Would that be so bad?"

His fingers stopped between her breasts. A thumb teased the flesh that rose above her lacy bra. Their eyes tangled wordlessly and they shared smiles that were so filled with love they were almost shy. "It would be wonderful. But sooner or later Maybelle might object."

The reminder that the Poppys now owned Barren Heath Isle was a harsh slap of reality. She sobered. "I suppose you're right." She watched his long fingers as they finished buttoning her blouse. "And Dana might miss you sooner or later." She managed a smile.

He looked up from his work. "I'm not sure about me, but I know she'd drive everybody nuts wanting to go find you." He helped her up. "When we tell her about us, she'll be sure you're marrying me just to please her."

"Well . . ." Mandy's smiled blossomed. "Maybe not just to please her. But we can keep that part our little secret." She pulled up on her toes and nuzzled his cheek, hugging him around the waist. "I can't figure out why I fought loving you so hard."

"Because you're a good, loyal woman who doesn't break commitments." He kissed her forehead. "It's a trait I plan to nurture in you."

She giggled at the sexy overtone of his words. "I'm crazy about the way you nurture." She lifted her head and gazed up at him. "Let's go get packed. We've got wild asses waiting at home."

He grinned lasciviously. Without need for words, he was telling her there were wild asses much nearer than that. She slapped his chest playfully. "Your mind is very dirty, Dr. Danforth."

His hearty laughter rang in the branches, frightening birds into flight.

"What's so humorous?" she asked, barely able to hide her smile.

"I didn't say a word."

"Then why am I blushing?"

He raised a quizzical brow. "To turn me on?"

She felt her skin flush as a new surge of longing filled her. How could he do that to her with a simple string of words? Until meeting Rule, she'd had no idea how arousing the English language could be. Wondering if her yearning was visible, she lowered her lashes.

"Rule..." she tried, but her throat was suddenly dry. She swallowed convulsively. "Don't talk that way if you want me to go. I'm only human."

He bent and kissed both eyelids in turn, a sweet, slow tribute to his love for her. "There's nothing 'only' about you," he assured quietly. Draping a possessive arm around her, he led her toward the garden's entrance. "And I never want you to go, at least not from me."

She reached up and laced her fingers with his. "Tell me, Rule," she asked, jubilant with joy. "Do New Mexico cowboys ever make love in a bed?"

He laughed. "I understand it's beginning to catch on."

She nestled her cheek against his chest. "No offense to Lydia's trysting place, but what do you think about trying it someday?"

Besides a rich chuckle that suggested strongly that her "someday" would not be long in coming, his only response was to squeeze her fingers in gentle understanding.

They walked in silence. Mandy slid an arm around his waist, hooking her thumb through a belt loop. She held on, enjoying the warm, male scent that filled her nostrils. She inhaled, recalling his naked arousal. The memory weakened her limbs and made her feel indecently damp. Her lips quirked with amusement at her unexpected but delightful reaction, and she sighed with happiness.

"Second thoughts?" he asked, sounding strangely guarded.

She blinked up to meet his gaze. He was regarding her with loving but solemn eyes. "Why would you ask that?"

"The sigh." He hugged her even closer. "I've been thinking. What about your work? Could you give that up?"

She supposed she shouldn't be surprised by the question. How could she expect a man with Rule's history to totally cast off his doubts so easily? She smiled, pulling him to her.

"Darling," she said, her voice muted with tenderness. "I don't know what I'll do about my work. It'll depend on where we go. But whatever I do, it will include you and Dana. If you want my promise in blood,

I'll bleed." A tear slid down her cheek and dangled from her chin before Rule wiped it away with his knuckles.

He took her face between his hands. "Don't bleed," he murmured, taking her lips and using them so well that when he, at last, released her, she could barely stand. He drew her beneath the shelter of his arm as they began to walk again.

She leaned against him and hung on to his belt, mumbling through thickened lips, "You make me all limp."

He chuckled. "Funny, you do just the opposite to me." He nudged her, graphically proving his point.

She moaned her delight and was about to suggest that they adjourn to the secret garden when a familiar voice interrupted from some distance away.

"Hey, there! Where've you two been?" Steppy asked. "I've been looking for you!"

Mandy heard Rule's groan as she stumbled unwillingly from his embrace. They cast pained, fleeting glances toward each other before facing Steppy, who was jogging down the path from the mansion. He was beaming. Mandy thought that odd, considering the fact that his most detested relative had beaten him out of an estimated six-hundred-million-dollar estate.

"You'll never believe it, Mandy!" he huffed, coming to a disjointed halt before them. "You'll never guess who just called me!" He clapped her sharply on the shoulders. "Hello, Danforth," he added without taking his eyes from Mandy's confused expression. "It was Ward Jamison, that's who. Your photographer friend. He wants to pay me for the use of my photographs in some book he's collaborating on—two thousand bucks! Think of it. Two thousand dollars just for using two pictures. He's not even buying them outright." He clapped her hard again, making her wince. "Pinch me. I know I'm dreaming."

"Why, that's wonderful, Steppy," she said, trying to ignore the throbbing in her arms where he was gripping her. "Which ones?"

"Oh, the bat and, of all things, Maybelle. Said the book was called *Things That Go Bump in the Night*— creepy stuff. Said with a subject like Maybelle, I could make a fortune. I told him so far that ugly mug of hers has just given me an acid stomach. Ward laughed. He wants me to call him Ward. Said he wants me to come out to his place. Meet him."

"I'm so happy for you, Steppy. But you might have a problem with Maybelle. You'll probably need a release from her for the use of her photograph."

Steppy laughed. "Oh, I got that right after you mailed the pictures off. I'm not as stupid as she thinks. I know something about the legalities of that sort of thing. When I asked her for the release, Maybelle said, and I quote, 'Paying me twenty-five bucks for my picture just proves to me how stupid you are, nephew. Consider the picture yours.' And she signed the release." He shook his head. "You shoulda heard her when I said I got a thousand bucks for that picture. My ears are still sizzling." He rolled his eyes theatrically.

"I'll bet—"

"I told Ward it'd be me and Savi coming to his home," he interrupted in an excited rush. "We're getting married just as soon as this hunt is over."

Mandy and Rule exchanged perplexed glances.

"Isn't the hunt over?" Rule asked.

It was Steppy's turn to look surprised. "Heck, no. Weren't you there when they opened that old metal trunk? Full of rusty pots and pans. Mr. Perth said Lydia'd stuck it out there as a joke." He laughed dryly. "That old lady had one weird sense of humor."

"That must have been hard on Maybelle," Mandy mused.

Steppy snorted. "Yeah. She was so brokenhearted that she stubbed her cigarillo out on Mr. Perth's sports coat. Last time I saw him, he and his shoulder pads were smoldering." Steppy shook his head.

"Sounds like Maybelle's had a lousy day," Rule observed quietly.

"I guess," Steppy remarked, appearing preoccupied. "I tell you, I'll be glad to get off this island and to some little loft apartment where I can work." He laughed. "May even pay Auntie Maybelle to sit for me." He snorted with humor. "Never thought I'd ever say that!"

"You don't sound as hellbent on finding the fortune, Steppy," Mandy remarked. "I'm surprised."

He stuffed his hands into his jeans pockets. Jeans had been a new addition to his wardrobe of late. Both he and Savina were dressing more like hippies of the 1960s than yuppies.

Shrugging bashfully, he told her, "My dad always said making money was the most important thing in life. I believed him—swallowed the whole dog-eat-dog package. Don't know why—he was always so miserable.

"Savina's folks were the same way, and she was never happy at home. We've sort of decided that maybe money isn't what's really important."

Mandy listened to his simple little recital, feeling happy for him and his recently cultivated insight. She could see in him a new strength of character beginning to develop. It was ironic, but sweet, that Savina had been the catalyst for such a positive change.

Steppy swung his arms wide, drawing her back to his words. "Savina thinks my pictures are worthwhile, and I love her for that. I love her for a lot of things—for telling me the truth about why she started out to help me in the first place—really took courage."

As he spoke, Mandy and Rule exchanged meaningful glances. So Steppy knew the truth? That was good.

"I'm almost afraid that if I find the fortune, I'll lose the hunger to create. I don't want to lose that any more than I want to lose Savi. . . ." He looked from Mandy to Rule, his expression wide-eyed and intent. "Does that make any sense?"

"It makes quite a bit of sense, Steppy," Mandy said, leaning up to graze a kiss on his jaw. "And congratulations on your engagement."

A ruddy blush reddened his face from his neck up past his thinning hairline. He grinned self-consciously.

"Where's the bride-to-be?" Rule asked.

He half turned. "Here she comes." He pulled a hand free from its denim casing and waved warmly. "Hi, Savi." Without dragging his eyes from his fiancée, he murmured in awe, "Isn't she pretty?"

Mandy watched Savina hurry toward them along the path. She was dressed in relaxed jeans and one of Steppy's button-down shirts, its tail irreverently knotted at her waist. But the most intriguing difference was the total lack of makeup. Her complexion was ivory pale and tinged only by the blush of happiness she exhibited as she neared Steppy.

Her eyes were a perky delight behind dainty lashes that suited her small features nicely. Her hair was straight and hung like silver silk past her shoulders. There was a whisper of darker hair at the roots, and Mandy thought Savina would be a rare, understated beauty when her natural color was restored.

"Hi, everybody," Savina greeted them happily, taking Steppy's arm in both of hers. "Did my little honey pie tell you the good news?" With their nods, she added, "I wasn't surprised. He's a genius with a camera lens."

"Oh, I thought you meant your engagement—or that the fortune hadn't been found," Mandy said.

"Oh, isn't it wonderful—our engagement, I mean." Savina gazed starry-eyed at Steppy. "We're not sure how we feel about the fortune anymore. Money can corrupt, you know."

Rule's brow lifted in amusement. "I've heard that rumor."

"Then you see our predicament."

Mandy glanced over at Rule. He was pursing his lips to mask his mirth. Taking his hand, she drew his attention. With laughing eyes, he winked at her, and her heart stumbled with happiness. Turning back to Savina, she offered, "Whatever you decide to do, we wish you luck."

Savina smiled genuinely. "Oh, we'll have luck. We have each other. Come on, honey. Fog's rolling in and I think you could get some really great—kinda eerie shots of me—you know—" she was pulling him along, and her voice was getting fainter, but she could still be heard as she finished "—lying naked across those rocks. Can't you just see it?"

Rule chuckled. "I can see it."

Mandy poked his ribs, eliciting a grunt from him as they watched Steppy tuck her beneath an arm. He was murmuring something, but it was indistinct.

"Have you ever seen anything like those two?" Mandy whispered, grinning.

"Maybe Annette Funicello and Frankie Avalon, but they were into gritty reality compared to these two."

"I'm happy for them." Mandy passed him a highly suggestive smile. Tugging him to her, she rubbed her hips seductively against his, whispering, "And I'm very, very happy for us. . . ."

"Well, well!" Maybelle bellowed. "This is exactly the sort of 'help' I'd guessed you'd been getting, Rule. I suppose she expects a slice of the fortune?"

Mandy's face blazed with humiliation and she tried to back away, but Rule held her to him. She looked up in time to see a flash of anger cross his face, but in an instant it was gone. He met his aunt's venomous gaze and replied with light sarcasm, "Why, hello, Maybelle. Your day's going well, I trust?"

She glared at him. "You know damned well how my day's going. Or you might, if your brains weren't throbbing in your pants."

Mandy stifled a gasp as Rule's arm tightened reassuringly about her. There was a disquieting pause while Rule eyed his aunt levelly. Mandy grew nervous, not wanting an ugly confrontation. She was about to suggest they leave when she saw Rule's lips open in a smile. It was directed at his aunt.

"You really are a feisty old cuss, aren't you?" he kidded, roguishly.

"What!" She bristled. "Why you . . ." She balled spindly fingers and shook a fist threateningly. "I'll fetch my whip and show you what I do to foul-mouthed young pups!"

Rule took Mandy's hand and drew her toward Maybelle. It surprised both women when he engulfed his aunt's thin shoulders with a congenial arm. "We need to get something straight, Maybelle," he remarked softly. "First, Mandy and I are not the enemy. And second, I know you're a whole lot more bark than you are bite. You're like a hungry dog, growling at strangers—not because you're mean, but because you're afraid."

"What! Why..." she blustered. "I've never been frightened a day in my life. I practically raised Arnold and Bessie. And I've spent over thirty years inside a cage with lions." She wagged a bony finger at his nose. "Don't you call me afraid, boy!"

"Sure, sure. I know. I also know it's tough to be alone—like I was when Doc took me in, or to be broke and getting along in years—like you and Henry."

Maybelle's eyes widened as he spoke. "It's not easy for retired people to make ends meet these days." Rule inclined his head toward Henry, who was having an animated conversation with Old Fatty, the rabbit. When Henry drew out a ticket and handed it toward the animal, it hopped away.

"You're not as strong as you used to be, and you've got a childlike husband to worry about. It's tough to be out of control, especially for somebody like you, Maybelle, who's always needed to be in control."

Mandy glanced up at his face and was touched by the gentleness there. He was speaking soothingly to this vicious woman as though she were a child who'd just awakened from a nightmare. "You're desperate to find the fortune because you're a proud woman, and you think it's your last chance to keep yourself and Henry from being hungry and homeless in your old age. Right?"

She stared daggers at him but said nothing.

He squeezed her shoulder, his smile kind. "Look, Maybelle. Don't worry so much. We're family, and families should stick together." He looked lovingly at Mandy. "We may not have much when this is over, but we'll do what we can to help. Right, Mandy?"

She smiled up at him and blew him a kiss.

Maybelle yanked away from him. "Henry and I don't want any handouts!"

"Did I say anything about a handout?" Rule straightened her pith helmet, which had gone askew on her head and grinned down at her. "Now I know where my daughter inherited her spunk—from her crusty old aunt. I don't know whether to kiss you or wring your neck."

She scowled at him, but it seemed more a look of curiosity than anger. "Sometimes you remind me of your father," she remarked tonelessly. "I didn't understand him, either."

"Mind if I take that as a compliment?"

She dropped her gaze, nimbly plucking a pack of cigarillos from her shirt pocket. After tapping the pack against her fist, she pulled out a thin cigar. "Suit yourself, boy," she muttered, before lighting it and taking a drag. After what seemed like a long time, she met his gaze again. Her look was guarded. "Sorry about that remark earlier, Danforth. Maybe you're not such a bad sort."

He smoothed a gray strand of hair behind her ear. "Maybe you aren't, either, you old fraud."

Maybelle made a disgusted face, but it lacked conviction. "Watch the nasty cracks." She took another drag. Though her lips were pursed tightly around the cigar, Mandy detected an odd quiver, as though she were on the verge of smiling. She blew smoke at them, remarking sharply, "Before this little scene gets too sickening, I'll deliver my message and get on with important business. That dimwit, Emma—she's in a snit."

Rule's expression lost its humor. "Is something wrong?"

With a dismissing gesture that drizzled ashes in the breeze, Maybelle explained. "It's nothing. Jetta used to wander off all the time when she was that age. She always turned up okay."

"What do you mean?" Mandy asked, her voice growing tight. "Is Dana missing?"

Maybelle's shrug confirmed it. "Emma said she left the child alone stirring cookie dough for a couple of minutes, and when she got back, the dough was spilled all over the floor and the child was gone."

Rule's expression hardened. Trying to quell her panic, Mandy forced a smile. "Dana's okay, Rule. I feel it," she lied. When his eyes clashed with hers, they were filled with alarm. He knew the dangers as well as she. It was nearing dusk and fog was rolling in. Before long, anyone crazy enough to be outside would be stumbling around blindly.

Mandy felt Rule's hand tighten around hers, and she knew he was thinking just what she was. God help them if Dana was wandering near the cliff!

MANDY GLANCED uncertainly around. Mist was snaking across the lawn toward the mansion. The cottage was little more than a phantomlike shape behind an undulating curtain of vapor.

"The cottage," Mandy cried, tension sharpening her tone. "She has to be there."

A moment later they were rushing through the screen door, rousing Josh from his nap. Groggy, he sat up on his elbows. A stack of dog-eared magazines toppled from his chest to the floor. "What's the ruckus?" he wheezed, fumbling to pull his glasses down from his forehead.

"Dana," Mandy called, flinging open her bedroom door and dashing inside to look around. "Has she been here? Have you seen her?

"No. But I've been snoozin'. Why?" With a supporting hand on the back of the couch, he pulled himself up. "Somethin' wrong, Rule?"

"Dana's lost, and a bad fog's rolling in," he supplied, his expression concerned.

"Lordie." Josh frowned, shaking his head. "You sure she ain't somewhere in the mansion? That's a big place."

Mandy hurried out of her room, nearly slamming into Rule. He caught her gently by the arms. "She's not here, Mandy. Maybe we ought to go up to the mansion. She could be there. Let's not panic."

"You're right," she acknowledged with a quick, edgy smile, trying to calm herself. "We'd best talk to Emma.

Start at the beginning. She's probably been located by now, anyway."

"Probably," he agreed, but his expression didn't mirror his optimistic response.

"I'll take a gander around the cottage," Josh offered, struggling to his feet. "Chuck me that cane, Mandy." He held out a quaking hand.

She hesitated. He was so frail. He didn't need to be tramping around in the damp. Still, she relented after only the briefest moment. Josh would never sit by idly while Dana was missing, bad heart or no bad heart. She grabbed up the cane from the floor beside the over-stuffed chair and took it to him. With a brief hug, she said, "Take it easy, will you?"

"Hush." He patted her shoulder. "I know this island blindfolded. I'll be fine. Now, you two git."

She nodded, relinquishing the scrawny shoulders. "Thanks, Papa Josh. We'll let you know."

Hand in hand they hurried down the path toward the mansion. The setting sun was shrouded behind a wall of clouds, and the fog was swelling, engulfing the mansion in gauzy oblivion.

Minutes later, Emma related her tearful story, pointing out the cookie dough that still spattered the floor. She told them she had servants searching the attic and all the bedrooms. No luck yet.

Mandy and Rule decided to search the unoccupied wing. Armed with a flashlight, they made quick work of the rooms and were at last in the storage room with the secret passage to the cavern below. They couldn't remember if it had been resealed.

When Rule directed his flashlight toward the corner where the medieval fireplace stood, they could see that it hadn't.

"Do you think she could have found her way down there?" Mandy asked.

"She's never been afraid of the dark. We'd better look."

They ducked into the hearth and carefully made their way down the warped and creaking steps. Rule called out Dana's name, but got no answer.

When they reached the bottom, both breathed a sigh of relief to see that she wasn't lying in an unconscious heap at the foot of the stairs. "Let's make a sweep of the perimeter," Rule suggested. "Just to be sure."

As they moved slowly around the oval cavern, they both called out Dana's name, not really expecting to get an answer at this point, but in desperate need of feeling as if they were doing something. Anything.

"Wait!" Mandy whispered, touching Rule's arm. "Listen."

They both went so still that they almost ceased breathing. At first Rule could hear nothing. He looked at Mandy. Her expression was intent, her head cocked toward the cement block barricade that separated the cavern from the cave beyond.

He listened for so long without hearing anything that the effort became almost painful. Then, when he was just about to ask Mandy what she'd thought she'd heard, he heard it, too.

The sound was high-pitched, and came in short bursts. Mandy and Rule looked at each other, their expressions perplexed. "What—" Mandy began, then cut herself off. The sound grew louder and became a quivery wail.

"It's Dana. She's crying," Mandy breathed.

Before she could say more, Rule called, "Dana, honey! It's Daddy. Are you all right?"

Silence.

"Dana!" he repeated, dropping to his knees next to the concrete and calling again. "Are you okay?"

Faintly, they heard an answer. It sounded like "Ooosss." It came again, this time with more strength. "Daddy. I'm lost!"

"It's okay, honey. Miss Mandy and I know where you are. Stay there. We're coming to get you. Do you hear me? Stay there!"

"Yes. Daddy? Hurry!" The whimpering began again, but neither Mandy nor Rule stayed to hear more. They bounded up the steps and were struggling down the slope toward the beach before either of them spoke again.

Panting from exertion, Mandy said, "Thank God she's all right. If she just stays there."

"She will," Rule gritted between clenched teeth, as if to make it so by the sheer force of his will. "She will, dammit."

Mandy swallowed hard, recalling Dana's stubborn nature. No one knew Dana better than Rule. She glanced over at him. He was holding the flashlight close to the ground so that they could watch their footing as they descended. His face was indistinct in the fog, but Mandy knew he must be praying that his daughter's budding independent spirit wouldn't be her undoing.

Once they reached the sand it was easier going, though slow. The fog was like chowder. Rule helped Mandy over some rocks that partially blocked the mouth of the cave. Once they were inside, they made quick work of the slippery cavern floor, deftly avoiding the gaping holes that shone up at them with reflected light, deceptively benign.

The farther they wound into the subterranean tunnel, the less fog they encountered. It was as though even the mist had grown frightened of becoming lost forever in these icy bowels.

They didn't dare call out Dana's name, for fear she'd run toward them, only to fall into one of the bottomless gashes in the rock and drown before they could reach her. They crept on steadily and as swiftly as they could until the hollow began to shrink in size. Rule was forced to crouch as they edged forward.

"Daddy!" Dana cried, jumping up when she saw their flashlight beam in the distance.

"Don't move," Rule cautioned, when he saw that she was just on the other side of a good-sized hole. "I'll get you."

Dana sat back down and clutched her stuffed zebra to her chest. Mandy noticed that she was wearing cowboy boots and the yellow dress. "Don't be afraid, Dana," she whispered soothingly. A moment later when they reached her, Mandy kneeled, hugging the child. "You okay?"

Dana pulled up on her knees and hugged Mandy back, bursting into tears. "I got mixed up—couldn't find the door out. I...wanted to see what a cave was...I...then ZeZe got dunked and all wet and heavy. Is ZeZe dead?"

As Rule bent down beside his daughter, Mandy was stroking her hair, crooning softly to her that ZeZe would be okay—that everything would be okay. When Dana's sobbing had dwindled to an occasional hiccup, Mandy sat back. For the first time, she realized that the back of her blouse was soaked where Dana had been dangling her toy.

She took the zebra from Dana, remarking brightly, "ZeZe is a real mess. But tomorrow he'll be just fine. We'll put him out in the sun and he'll be good as new."

Dana sniffed, looking from Mandy to her father. Her eyes were wide with concern. "Daddy. I spilled the cookies." She hiccupped and wiped her nose with the back of her hand. "And I came to see the cave without your 'mission—and I dunked ZeZe and got lost." She pulled the toy from Mandy's hand and pressed it protectively to her chest, squeezing water into her lap. "Are you gonna spank me?"

Rule's eyes were tender and filled with relief as he looked down at his daughter. Her face was tear-stained, her body shivering from the cavern's chilly temperature. He exhaled heavily. "For coming down here, I should turn you over my knee, young lady, and plaster your backside."

"No," she said pouting, sidling over to him on her knees and handing him her zebra. "Spank ZeZe. She told me to. ZeZe wanted to see a cave."

"Oh, *she* did?" he asked, lifting an amused brow. "Maybe I'd better not let ZeZe play with you anymore if she's going to get you into trouble. What do you think?"

Dana grabbed it back, squeezing it to her. "*No*, Daddy! Please. ZeZe wasn't really bad." She dropped her head dejectedly to her chin and whispered pitifully, "Spank me. I—I did it by myself."

The toy was soaking Dana's dress, and her teeth had begun to chatter. With a tired smile, he said, "Well, as long as you admit it, I won't this time. But remember, young lady, this is a very dangerous place. You and ZeZe were very lucky you weren't hurt. Now give me that thing before you catch pneumonia." He took ZeZe from her and frowned. "How did this get so wet?"

Mandy took Dana by the hand and they stood as she explained, "It was dark. I fell—I dunked ZeZe."

They skirted the jagged hole that very easily could have taken Dana's life. Mandy tried to shrug off the horrible thought. Grasping for any conversational straw, she offered offhandedly, "Now ZeZe knows how a doughnut feels."

"A doughnut?" asked Dana, her face pinched in confusion. "What does she mean, Daddy?"

Rule lifted Dana up into his arms. After handing Mandy the flashlight, he draped his free arm about her as they walked. "You know the way ol' Mike dunks his cornbread in buttermilk?"

Mandy made a face at the very thought while Dana nodded.

"Well," Rule went on. "Some people dunk their doughnuts in milk or coff—"

"That's it!" Mandy heard her own voice ring out and echo back at her in the narrow chamber. Whirling to face Rule, she cried, "'A doughnut's fate.' Remember, Rule? That was one of the clues."

He glanced down at her, squinting against the semidarkness. "You're saying, being dunked is the doughnut's fate Lydia was suggesting?"

"It could be."

He studied her face. Her eyes were large and very bright in their excitement. He found the picture wholly charming. With a potent grin, he suggested, "Maybe we should go inspect the coffeepot."

She stared at him, feeling an odd catch in her chest. She wondered if he had any idea how that crooked smile affected her. Their gazes held meaningfully before hers slid away. With a wry smile, a slow headshake, she said, "Go ahead and tease, but Lydia dunked her doughnuts, and I'm beginning to have a gut feeling. . . ." She swung the flashlight around, illuminating the damp stone surrounding them. "Walls, Rule. 'Walls where no walls stand.'" She frowned in thought. "Oh, I can't think. What were the other clues?"

His expression grew thoughtful as he scanned her fine-boned features. "'Down, down, down.'"

"We're down." She began to pace nervously.

"'Lost and green.'"

She swung the light around. "The walls are gray." She chewed on her lip as she prowled. "Doesn't fit."

"The water's green," Rule said quietly, halting her in her tracks. She slanted the beam downward, and they both stared.

"It can't be down there," Mandy mused, not realizing she was even talking aloud. "What are some of the other clues?"

"The first one was 'A square within a circle.'" Their gazes leaped together as he urged, "Are any of these holes perfectly round?"

Mandy swallowed. Her throat was prickly dry. "I—I don't know. Oh, Rule, do you think . . . ?"

He scanned the floor of the cave suspiciously. "I don't dare, but let's look around."

After returning to where they'd found Dana, they began moving toward the cave's mouth, methodically scanning the water-filled holes on the pitted floor of the cave.

"Daddy? What are you looking for?" Dana asked in a reverent, almost frightened, whisper.

"A round hole," he smiled reassuringly at her wide-eyed expression.

Anxiously, Mandy glanced their way, whispering, "Like that one?" Rule turned in the direction Mandy had cast the flashlight beam. They stared at the still, green water as it reflected the light back up at them—from within a perfectly round opening in the rock.

"Like that one," Rule repeated, his voice hushed. His gaze snapped up to meet Mandy's. There was total disbelief in her face.

"Could it be?" she whispered.

Kissing his daughter's cheek, Rule said, "I'm going to set you down, Dana. And I don't want you to move from this spot. Do you understand?"

When she'd nodded somberly, Rule deposited her against the wall, insisting that she sit quietly while they decided on their next move.

Turning back, he asked Mandy, "Is this one of the bottomless ones?"

She shook her head regretfully. "I don't know."

"It's about two feet wide. Pretty narrow for much of a treasure chest." He lay down on one side. "If it's deeper than I can reach with one arm, we're going to have a problem."

"That's scummy-looking water." She knelt down beside him, her face pinched with disgust as he plunged his arm in.

He was up to his shoulder, fishing around when he grinned at her. "What do your guts say now?"

She shrugged lamely. "My guts are numb. Can you touch bottom?"

He shook his head and drew up to a sitting position. "Too deep, and it's too narrow for me to fit in." Squeezing water from his shirtsleeve, he asked, "Any suggestions?"

Mandy looked away from the rippling water and then forced her gaze back. Her stomach lurched. She wondered what the stuff was that was floating on the surface, and what was worse, what there might be eyeing her hungrily from underneath? She didn't want to think what they were both thinking, but she realized their options were pretty slim. With a nervous swallow, she said, "I guess—I'm pretty small...."

A smile played at the corners of his mouth. "You're pretty, period." Their eyes held, and Mandy's skin flushed, warming her against the cave's chill.

She let an edgy laugh slip out, adding, "And I think in a few seconds, I'm going to be pretty wet."

He stood, touching her hand. "I'll hold you. If you don't feel the bottom right away, I'm pulling you up. Got it?"

She sucked in a steadying breath. "Got it."

With Rule holding her arms, she dropped down into the pool, allowing herself only one sharp gasp as the cold water crept up her thighs.

"Like a cold shower?" he asked, his eyes glinting with amusement.

An unwilling smile crooked her lips. "That's right. Hit me when I'm down."

Smelly water lapped her chin, and she strained to touch bottom. "I don't feel anything," she croaked.

Rule's expression was concerned. "I don't know, Mandy. This may be a fool's errand. Maybe you'd better—"

She didn't wait to hear more. This could be their chance, and she wasn't going to let it slip by just because she was a freezing coward. She ducked her head beneath the surface, catching Rule unaware, and stealthily slipped from his grasp. Grabbing a slimy rock she pushed herself down through the icy water.

When her tennis shoes rammed forcefully into the bottom it almost made her lose her breath. The pool must have been about seven or eight feet deep.

She still had plenty of air, but she was beginning to shiver violently from the extreme cold. She forced herself to stay under by clutching outcroppings of rock as she felt along the bottom with her feet.

It surprised and frightened her for an instant when Rule's hand closed around her wrist, tugging gently. She let go of the rock with that hand and patted his forearm reassuringly, continuing to move her feet, first checking the center, then carefully scraping the surface toward the perimeter.

She shuddered convulsively, knowing that soon both her body heat and her oxygen would be dangerously depleted, but she was determined to get this done in one try. She never wanted to do this again!

Her foot snagged something soft. Soft? "*Yuck!*" she groaned through a flurry of escaping bubbles. Not caring to dwell on what horrible things trapped in cave water—either dead or living—might be soft, she hooked the toe of each sneaker around two sides of it and slowly, so not to dislodge the object, began to move upward.

As soon as Rule realized what she was doing, he pulled her along. When her face surfaced, she took a huge gulp of air and looked up into a blur. Two blurs. "Are you okay?" Rule asked as Mandy brushed water from her eyes. She blinked up at them. Both Dana and Rule were frowning, looking extremely worried.

"Rule, I've got something," she spluttered, unable to staunch the shivering that engulfed her body. "Pull me up very carefully so I don't drop it."

He reached down and grasped her under the arms, asking, "Where is it?"

"Between m-my feet. It's too narrow to reach down and g-get."

"You're frozen solid," he moaned, lifting her until she was settled on the edge. Quickly, she grabbed a black, shiny bundle from between her calves and handed it to him. "What d-do you think about my guts n-now?" she crowed, her face animated with victory.

"I say if you and your guts don't get warm and dry pretty quickly, they won't be worth much on the open market." He laid the dripping package aside and stripped off his shirt, draping it across her trembling shoulders. "Let's get out of here."

As he pulled her to her feet, she protested feebly, "Don't you want to s-see what's in it?"

He hoisted Dana on one hip and looked Mandy's shuddering frame up and down with a worried frown. Handing her the package she'd dredged up, he said, "Sure, I want to know what it is. But it can wait until a couple of females I know thaw out."

On quivering limbs, Mandy was practically dragged to the cave opening. Fog, damp and cold greeted them with clammy breath. The going along the beach was neither easy nor warm. At last, they struggled up to the rise where the cottage was perched. Toasty light spilled from a window, penetrating the gloomy night. Exhausted, sopping wet and choked with anticipation, they headed toward it.

FIFTEEN MINUTES LATER, Mandy was wrapped in a lusciously warm terry robe, her hair clean and towel-dried. Dana could be heard humming, splashing around happily in a warm tub, and Josh, relieved that the child had been found, had fallen into an exhausted sleep on the couch.

Mandy looked up as Rule reentered the cottage. He grinned down at her as she sat at the kitchen table. "I told Emma we have Dana. She was relieved, to say the least."

"Good. Well," Mandy asked in a small voice, "what do you think we have here?"

The wrapped box was sitting in the middle of the kitchen table. Rule sat down across from Mandy and picked it up, fingering it. "Could be another one of Lydia's red herrings."

Mandy nodded, her mouth a grim line. "I know."

"What do you bet it's Jimmy Hoffa's cremated remains?" he teased.

"If it is, it's going back," she retorted. Dragging her gaze from the box, she eyed him narrowly. "Do you want me to have a heart attack? Open it," she gritted under her breath.

His eyes glittered with humor. "I bet you're hell to live with on Christmas Eve."

Exasperated but unable to hide a smile at the delicious thought of living with this man, she grabbed the box from him. "Just wait till I get you alone, buster." She looked around to see if they'd disturbed Josh. He was snoring softly. "You'll pay for this torture."

"Promises, promises." His tone turned her stomach into a fluttery mass.

Trying to ignore the erotic pull of his presence across the table, she began to scrape away at one end of the electrician's tape that swathed the black plastic. After a minute without success, Rule relieved her of the package and sliced away at the tape with the sharp blade of a pocket knife.

He proceeded to peal off six layers of waterproof material. All the time he worked, Mandy's heart was lodged in a heavy lump halfway down her throat. After what had seemed like days of waiting Rule pulled out an antique china box, its lid inlaid with semiprecious gems.

"How lovely," Mandy breathed. "If it's a joke, at least it's more tasteful than the last one."

Rule set the fragile box on the table and gently lifted the lid. Inside was nothing but a folded piece of paper. Mandy raised her eyes to Rule's, her hope waning. Trying to be positive, she said, "Maybe it's a treasure map." She couldn't think of a single reason to keep smiling, but she did.

Rule must have sensed her growing doubt, because he reached across the table and covered her cool hand with his. It was a haven—warm, solid and radiating his love. "Mandy, I want you to know that finding you has been my treasure. Whatever this says, it won't affect that."

Sweet tears stung her eyes and she grew strangely calm. He was right. They had found each other. Knowing that, she knew everything else would fall into its proper place, treasure or no treasure. Nodding, she said, "Open it."

When he unfolded the page, a small, brass key fell out, clanking on the tabletop and startling them. Mandy picked it up and turned it in her hand. It looked as if it belonged to a safe-deposit box. She could do nothing but stare blankly at it as Rule read the note scrawled in a feathery script.

"'If you be man, go first and buy you a woman of wit and fancy as Arnold did. You shall never be bored. If you be woman with enough wile to beat me at my game, then with my fortune, you truly have everything. Enjoy!'"

With my fortune? Truly have everything? Enjoy? As the full implication of the note sank in, Mandy dragged her eyes from the key to fix her disbelieving gaze on Rule's face. His smile was hypnotically tender, his eyes soft. She couldn't believe he loved her as much as his eyes told her he did. That truth was harder to comprehend than the fact that they'd actually discovered Lydia's treasure.

"Welcome home, darling," he whispered, his voice underscored with desire.

A trembling began in her fingers and whispered through her body to settle deep inside her. Wanting terribly to take him inside her, but knowing Josh and Dana would no doubt be shocked by the scene, she squelched her longing—for the moment—and reached across the table, winnowing the hair at his temple. "I love you so much," she whispered, her voice breaking with emotion.

He covered her hand with his and kissed the sensitive underside of her wrist. With their shared smiles, they promised each other that the night to come would be one of unequaled celebration, but it would be a very private affair.

13

IT WAS LATE MORNING. Mr. Perth had requested everyone's presence in the dining room for an announcement. Maybelle puffed agitatedly at her cigar. Steppy, to her right, draped his arm over the back of Savina's chair and whispered in her ear, eliciting breathless giggles from her. Rule grinned at them. They were totally oblivious to anything or anyone else. He knew how they felt, but he hoped he didn't look quite as sappy as Steppy did. Then again, to hell with how he looked. He was a damned happy man. Mandy would soon be his wife.

Henry sat humming something that sounded like "Itsy Bitsy Spider," while he danced his fingers around on the tablecloth. Henry Poppy was clearly a happy man, too.

Jetta sat to Rule's right, toying with a bracelet. Mandy, who'd joined them this morning, was on his left. She sat quietly, looking serene, but Rule knew she was nervous about being here. He bent near her ear and whispered, "How're you doing?"

She started, then smiled at him. "Okay, I guess. I just wish Mr. Perth didn't have to make such a production out of this."

"Apparently it was written into the will this way."

Mandy sighed, wondering where Lydia's lawyer was.

"So, just what is this important meeting, anyway?" Maybelle barked, making Mandy jump. "We're wasting valuable search time." She scowled at Mandy. "And what is that woman gardener doing here?"

She blanched, but Rule said simply, "Mandy is my fiancée." He squeezed her hand where it rested intimately on his thigh. "Since this is a family meeting, she has every right to be here."

Maybelle raised a string-thin brow and sneered. "Fiancée? You, too, Rule? I knew Steppy was a fool, and his empty head could be turned by a gold digger, but I thought you—"

"Maybelle," Rule interrupted tersely, "I told you once we were family, and family should stick together. Don't mess it up now."

Apparently the steely edge in Rule's voice had made an impression. Though she eyed them both with suspicion, Maybelle wisely chose to puff quietly on her cigar and keep any further observations to herself.

Even Steppy and Savina had gone quiet in the wake of Rule's warning. Both of them wore tiny smiles of satisfaction at Maybelle's humbling but said nothing.

The tinkle of Jetta's bangle bracelet drew everyone's attention as she smoothed back her hair. She looked up to see all eyes on her and laughed hollowly. "Why do I have the feeling this show's about to close?"

Just then Mr. Perth swept into the room, dressed as impeccably as usual in a black three-piece suit, starched white shirt and maroon tie. He stood aside to allow two servants to place a large metal box on the table.

"Oh-oh," Jetta murmured.

"What do you mean by that?" challenged Maybelle through a haze of smoke.

"Somebody's found something," Jetta said, looking around. "The party's over. I know it."

"Oh, you're such a gloom and doomer, Jetta," Maybelle growled. "Where you get it from, I'll never know."

Jetta burst out laughing. "Oh, mother, you're priceless."

Ignoring Jetta, Maybelle turned her attention to Mr. Perth. "What is this meeting all about, and what is that box for?" she demanded.

The servants exited before Mr. Perth faced Lydia's relatives. Solemnly he placed his hands on the mirrored surface of the box in front of him.

He cleared his throat importantly. "This is Lydia's safe-deposit box. It's been in a vault in the Portland Security Bank, but because of a—" he allowed himself a pregnant pause "—development, I had it brought over to the island this morning."

"I knew it," Jetta sighed. "Somebody found something, and it damned well wasn't me."

"This key—" Mr. Perth reached inside his coat and pulled out the brass key that Mandy and Rule had found "—was brought to me last night. I was told by the discovering party—or parties—that it was located in the place where Lydia herself placed it. It opens this box, and grants the owner—or owners—"

"*Blast it*, man!" Maybelle pounded the table with her fist. "Quit your babbling and tell us who found it before I strangle you with my bare hands."

Mr. Perth scowled at her but continued as though she hadn't spoken. "Owner—or owners—of the key the right to Lydia's entire fortune of six hundred and eighty-seven million dollars. Of course that is a conservative estimate, considering the spiraling value of gold, art, etcetera—"

"I'm going to *kill* him!" Maybelle stubbed her cigar into shreds.

"Mandy found the key in a small china box in a pool of water in the cave," Rule supplied quietly.

When all eyes turned to Mandy, she blushed furiously.

"I cry foul! She is an interloper and a troublemaker," Maybelle objected, standing up with such force that her chair toppled over backward. "She has no right!"

Mr. Perth paled at the outburst, but he composed himself swiftly. "I was given to understand that both Rule Danforth and Mrs. McRae retrieved the key together. Lydia made no provisions against people teaming up." He reached across Jetta and handed the key to Rule. "Would you care to do the honors, Mr. Danforth?"

Rule helped Mandy to her feet and they both circled to the head of the table where Rule handed Mandy the key. He grinned down at her. "You were the one who took the cold dip. You do the honors."

With trembling fingers, she unlatched the large box.

"I'll contest! I'll have this whole farce—"

"Oh, shut up and sit down, Aunt Maybelle," Steppy said, sounding more tired than irritated. He got up and righted her chair and then with a firm hand pushed her into it. "If you open your mouth again I, personally, will help you leave—through a closed window. Is that understood?"

Maybelle slapped his hand away and adjusted her helmet. "So it takes the specter of poverty to make you show a little backbone!" She sniffed disdainfully. "You're a great disappointment to me."

Steppy laughed. "Coming from you, that's a rare compliment."

"Oooooooh, how beauteous," Henry cried, clasping his hands together in delight as Mandy pulled a diamond-and-amethyst encrusted crown from the box. Following that came a necklace with row after scalloped row of sparkling diamonds, interspersed with dangling amethysts. The piece was so large that it could have been worn by a woman naked from the waist up and she would have been adequately covered to go out in public.

Mandy lifted out two similarly jeweled cuffs, each six inches long. Wi :. each piece that appeared, Jetta moaned as though in pain. When the last piece was revealed, her reaction was the same. It was a ring with a central amethyst the size of a walnut. Encircling it was a glittering band of square-cut diamonds, each at least three carats in weight.

Mandy had never seen the like—never even imagined that such opulent jewelry existed. Leave it to Lydia to own something so ostentatious. "I wonder if she ever wore these?" she whispered to Rule.

He chuckled. "Probably just for intimate little coronations around the house."

"Lord," Jetta breathed in awe. "They must be worth millions."

Mr. Perth pulled a notebook from his breast pocket. "Eleven million," he supplied, flipping the page. "They were once owned by Elizabeth I."

"Oh, Lizzy, baby," Jetta sighed. "Consider me your number-one fan!"

Rule whispered something to Mandy. When she smiled up at him and nodded, he picked up the crown and handed it to Jetta. Her expression clouded with confusion. "We want you to have this. Build your resort."

She was speechless as she stared at the crown. "I—I don't get it."

"Yes you do. Rule and I decided last night after Mr. Perth told us the contents of the box." Mandy slipped the ring on Jetta's limp finger. "You not only get the crown but the necklace and cuffs, too. And the ring. With our best wishes."

Jetta looked down at the huge cluster of precious stones, flashing silver and lilac fire on her finger. When she looked back up, she had tears in her eyes. The look touched Mandy. She knew that Jetta didn't soften easily.

"You two . . . What can I say?"

Rule smiled. "Break a leg."

Jetta winked. "You got a deal, cowboy."

"Why her?" Maybelle broke in hotly. "She's never been anything but a disobedient, headstrong little pain in my—"

"Mother . . ." Jetta fluttered her fingers toward Maybelle. "Kiss my amethyst!"

Rule pulled out a savings book and leaned over the table to hand it to Maybelle. "To answer your question, Maybelle, we gave it to her because families stick together."

Maybelle snatched up the book and eyed it with dark skepticism. "What's this? Some kind of cruel joke?"

Rule's smile turned melancholy. "That's up to you."

"Hell, mother, he doesn't have to give you anything, you know," Jetta muttered as she settled the crown on her head. "You could try saying thank you for a change of pace."

Maybelle had frozen, her widened eyes glued to the final page of the savings book.

"What is it?" Jetta asked in the middle of placing a cuff around one wrist. "Somebody give mother a slap on the back. I don't think she's breathing."

"My pleasure," Steppy offered, pounding away. "Maybelle, dear—" he seemed almost concerned "—come out, come out wherever you are." He looked up and grinned. "What am I saying? I've prayed for her to go catatonic for years."

"Ten and a half million dollars," Maybelle croaked, dropping the book to the tabletop. "I've never seen so many zeros. . . ."

"Holy Toledo!" Jetta tugged on Rule's belt. "That's damned decent of you two, considering everything."

"I'm sure she'd have done the same for me," Rule offered with a twinkle in his eye.

"Sure she would." Jetta grinned. "And Skizzo the Great has a shot at Secretary of Defense. Dream on."

"Look, Skizzo." Maybelle unsteadily pushed herself up to stand. "We can build our retirement home for circus folks—like old Jocko and the Square Man."

"We can?" His protruding little eyes widened.

"Yes, my pumpkin." She picked up the savings book and slipped it into her shirt pocket.

"Oh, joy!" He scooped up a fork. "I must start digging at once!"

"No, not here," she corrected. "We must go to our room and plan." As he leaped obediently from his chair, she added, her voice deadpan, as though she were in a state of shock, "We'll have a petting zoo. One-legged Eddie can run it. He'll feel so useful. . . ."

"And a matinee?" Henry squealed. "Can we have a matinee?"

They were walking out of the room, their backs to everyone else. Maybelle patted her husband on his bowler hat. "Of course we shall, my kingly sprite. Of course we shall."

Maybelle and her husband disappeared around the corner, Henry's high-pitched giggles growing dimmer but no less delighted.

Jetta rolled her eyes. She turned to Rule and Mandy. "I don't know about you people, but I was touched by their outpouring of gratitude." She fastened the necklace about her slender neck. "Well, I'm on pins and needles. What do Steppy and Savina get—California?"

"We don't want anything," Steppy said, looking earnest.

"That's right," Savina added fervently, clutching his arm to her breasts. "We have everything we need. We have each other."

"We'd like to give you a wedding gift," Mandy said. "Rule and I discussed it last night and—"

"Not necessary," Steppy assured her.

Rule pulled a folded slip of paper from his shirt pocket and reached over to hand it to Steppy. "Consider it a loan."

Steppy unfolded the paper. His expression grew puzzled. "This looks like a map."

Rule's grin was lopsided. "It is."

"Where does it lead?" Savina asked, her eyes wide with curiosity.

"To a secret garden." Rule took Mandy's hand in his, saying, "I think you'll know what to do when you get there."

Steppy and Savina exchanged speculative glances, looking perplexed. "Okay," Steppy said, smiling meekly. "Thanks." Still appearing baffled, they left the dining room hand in hand.

"A secret garden?" Jetta asked, standing and steadying her crown on her head. "It must be some special garden."

Mandy shared a brief glance with the man she loved and smiled at Jetta's understatement. The beauty of what she and Rule had found there rushed back into her mind's eye. Her face burned with the heat of her memories as she turned back to face Jetta.

Rule said, "I expect someday when you've squeezed all the fun out of being a wealthy woman, you'll find the time to discover a similar garden of your very own." He smiled kindly. "Your garden probably won't even be a garden."

She cocked her head curiously. "Going cryptic on me, huh? Well—" she wagged her ring at them "—I'm sure it'll all become clear to me someday. Meanwhile I think I'll go pack my goodies. I've got some moving and shaking to do."

After she'd swished rhythmically out the door, Mandy and Rule were left with only Mr. Perth. He had stood silently throughout the proceedings, his mouth gaping at the generosity he'd witnessed. Finally, he said, "In all my years as an attorney, I've never seen anything like this. Usually relatives bicker and claw over every penny."

Rule smiled. "Remember, we Danforths operate a brick short of a load."

Mr. Perth revealed his teeth in a smile. "I think not. At least not all the Danforths." He grew serious. "If I may be of any further service . . ."

Rule placed a comradely hand on his shoulder. "I'll get back to you after our honeymoon, Gavin. I have some legal papers I'd like you to draw up."

"I'll be waiting to hear from you."

With that, he left Mandy and Rule alone. They shared a gentle gaze for a long moment before Rule bent to place a kiss on the tip of her nose. "I think that went fairly well, don't you? No one slit anyone's throat."

She nuzzled his chest. "I'm glad it's over. But I still wish we could have done more for Steppy."

"We will," he murmured against her hair.

She looked up at him. "We will?"

He smiled. "I'll tell you later. What do you think Josh and Dana are doing?"

"He said he was going to start reading *Swiss Family Robinson* to her. He used to love to take Rebecca in his lap and read to her until she fell asleep. They're both probably asleep by now."

Rule draped a loving arm around her shoulders and led her from the dining room. "He has a granddaughter again. That'll be good medicine for him."

Mandy toyed with a button on his shirt. "You know what he said this morning?"

"What?"

"That pipe smoke isn't good for a little girl's lungs, so he's decided to quit smoking his pipe. Isn't that wonderful?"

"I'm glad to hear it. He's a great old man. And—" he hesitated for an instant before going on "—Peter must have been a good man, too, to have been loved by you."

Mandy stumbled to a halt and looked up at him. "That was a very generous thing to say."

He shrugged. "Just making peace with the dead." He squeezed her shoulder and led her toward the staircase, whispering, "Josh, Peter and I—we're all lucky to have had you in our lives."

"Thank you, sweetheart." She reached up and kissed his jaw. "Where are we going?"

"Upstairs."

Hiding a knowing smile, she put an arm about his waist, hugging him to her. "What's up there?"

"Guess." Sweeping her into his arms, he teased her with his eyes. "I think making love in a bed just may catch on."

"You think so?" She nipped at his jaw before trailing very inspiring kisses down his neck. "Do you know what I just realized?"

"That you love me above all other men?"

A merry giggle bubbled in her throat. "No, silly."

"Thanks a lot."

"I said *just* realized," she reminded him with a shy smile. "Seriously—" she tempted the hollow of his throat with her darting tongue "—I just realized that your whole life is dedicated to procreation—breeding—*sex*, if you will."

He chuckled. "I never thought of it quite that way."

"You know what?" Her cool hand slid beneath his shirt, her fingers stroking, delighting his flesh.

"I couldn't even guess," he growled seductively, his body responding quickly to her touch.

"You're *very* good at what you do."

Their eyes met. It was a gentle mingling, but one of unimaginable power. He gazed down at her, his expression tender and hungry at the same time. Almost too softly to be heard, he whispered, "Never walk away from me, Mandy."

"Oh, Rule—" her voice broke "—I could no more leave you than I could—" she cast around for something totally impossible "—than I could play a violin solo with the New York Philharmonic."

When her remark penetrated, his lips twitched with wry humor. "The chances are that remote?"

"You know," she said, a smile quivering on her lips. "The violinist in me is insulted that you were so quickly reassured by that."

"I'm sorry. I'm a cad." His eyes glinted with a mixture of humor and passion.

She allowed her hand to trail down until her fingertips had reached his jeans. "Take me to bed, you cad."

Her voice, so soft and intimate, went through him like flickering heat. He carried her up the stairs, his stride determined as he reminded her huskily, "I love you, Mandy."

She felt a luscious quiver inside. "You'd better," she said through a sigh. "You're going to have me around a long, long time." Luxuriating in his soft smile, she relaxed against him. Very soon they would both be soaring heavenward.

Epilogue

FEELING RESTLESS, Rule pushed through the double
doors that led out onto the balcony of his bedroom. It
was growing dusk, and the yacht hadn't yet returned
from the mainland. Mandy had gone in to Portland
early this morning. Rule had been busy in the meadow
all day, supervising the construction of the solar-heated
shelters that would house his equids during cold
weather. His work crews were on schedule, but there
was much to be done before the animals arrived next
month. But now, with the day's work completed and
night settling in, he was beginning to feel a gnawing
absence.

He looked out over the darkening ocean, scanned the
cliff off to his right, and then his gaze trailed up the bluff
to where the cottage sat. He could just barely see Josh,
napping on his porch swing, and he smiled. His eyes
drifted back to gaze fondly at the circular little garden
that had served as their wedding chapel. He and Mandy
had been married on the third of July. He chuckled to
himself. This past Fourth of July would be one neither
he nor Mandy would ever forget. The memory of their
wedding night sent a surge of raw hunger through his
belly that had nothing to do with the fact that he'd
worked through dinner.

He loved her so much. Mandy Danforth. His wife, the part of him that believed in forever, and was teaching him to believe in it, too. . . .

"Hi there, handsome," whispered a soft voice at his back as silky arms encircled his waist. "A penny for your thoughts."

He grinned, turning within her embrace to pull her yielding body into his. "I didn't hear you come in." His words were muted with tenderness as he inhaled the familiar, arousing scent of her hair. "I was beginning to worry."

She deftly teased the top button of his shirt loose and nuzzled the furred chest. "Busy day. For one thing, I got Dana enrolled in public school. Remember that quaint little school house up the coast? The one with its own dock? Apparently Dana won't be the only child going to school on a boat." Nipping playfully at his chest, she elicited a grunt from him.

"Ouch. You little cannibal," he rebuked lightly.

"That's me," she teased. "And I think it's only fair to warn you. I'm starving. You'd better run for your life."

His grin was breathtaking as he swept her up in his arms, carried her to the huge four-poster bed and dumped her unceremoniously there. "Have you no shame, woman?" As she lay on her back, smiling coyly up at him, he dragged the tail of his shirt from his jeans and discarded the garment on the floor. "A man works hard all day and then is expected to drop everything—" he sat down with his back to her and tugged off his boots and socks as he chided "—to satisfy a sexual whim of some dainty piece of fluff that wanders in at her convenience after a day of shopping and heaven knows what other diversion in the big city?"

He peered over his shoulder lifting a querulous brow, but his eyes were gleaming with passion.

She stared up at him guilelessly and then smiled, beginning to unbutton her blouse. "I'm ashamed of myself," she whispered, lowering her lashes demurely. "If I were you, I'd have absolutely nothing to do with me from now on." Splaying her blouse open to reveal milky breasts, barely concealed behind a transparent froth of lace, she added sweetly, "It's all I deserve."

Rule's gaze roamed lazily from the rounded loveliness of her breasts back up to her face before he crawled onto the bed, sprawling half on top of her, his naked chest crushing the softness he adored. He studied her face from a very close distance. At his unblinking perusal, she flushed a delicate shade of pink.

"You, Mrs. Danforth, are beyond redemption. Where, may I ask, did you learn such wanton ways?"

His breath was soft and welcome in her hair. "You know the answer to that," she said in a small, quavery voice.

The lines of his face were supple and gentled in a smile. "Do you realize it's our anniversary?"

He was brushing the barest rise of her breast with his thumb, rubbing back and forth, back and forth. Mandy smiled with the familiar sensation of urgency budding within her. "Yes," she breathed, her eyes shining. "It seems more like two minutes than two weeks."

"Mmm," he agreed, lightly kissing one luscious corner of her mouth.

"Speaking of anniversaries—" she kissed him back "— I picked up the mail. There was lots of news. Savina and Steppy've bought a farm in Vermont. He's sold several more photographs. They wanted to thank you for the trust you set up for them, but they plan to keep it intact for their children. Steppy says they want ten."

Rule grinned, kissing the other corner of her mouth. "They're turning into real earth children."

His thumb had slid beneath the lace, awakening delightful sensations in her nipple. "And... and," she sighed, closing her eyes, "Maybelle and Henry have picked the location for their circus-folk retirement home. Coon Springs, Idaho. Apparently the residents were very nice to them when their circus passed through the town once. Maybelle even broke down and thanked you for the money you gave them to build it."

Rule nuzzled her neck, making her shiver in response. His voice was hoarse as he muttered against her tingling skin. "I pity the Coon Springites. Their kindness won't go unpunished."

Mandy giggled, circling his firm, warm back with her hands. Running an inquisitive finger down his spine, she added, "Oh, and Jetta wrote to say she's found two 'controllable, dumb, but rich' partners who're buying into her resort property deal."

"She means two men," Rule said with a chuckle. "Jetta is quite a woman. She'll be wealthy in her own right someday."

Mandy's hand had reached the barrier of Rule's jeans. Undaunted, she slid her fingers beneath the denim in search of choicer game. "Jetta's got quite a man for a cousin," she whispered. "To give each of the losers a share of the fortune. That was wonderful of you."

Rule's answer was a muffled groan.

She stifled a giggle, feigning worry. "Is something wrong, darling?"

"You're a funny woman," he growled, lifting his head to frown down at her. But his eyes told her he was a man well satisfied with his lot in life. "You're going to force me to take action."

"Take it," she sighed, her hand sliding lower, to cup a well-muscled buttock. "Take me..."

He groaned, pulling up on one elbow to shed his jeans. As he unbuckled his belt, his eyes caught on an unexpected object lying above them on the pillow. It was Dana's zebra. He picked it up. "What is this doing in here?"

Unable to restrain her desire, Mandy began to unzip his jeans. "Dana gave it to me when I met her on her way out to visit Josh. She said she was going to play with Old Fatty, and that ZeZe was a baby and needed to go to bed. She asked me to put him . . . her away."

Rule's brows lifted in surprise, and he laid the toy aside.

"It's a good sign," Mandy said. "She's got a home, now. . . ."

"And a mother," Rule added, smiling down at her.

Mandy nodded. "She doesn't need substitutes anymore."

Rule's gaze grew bold and full of promise. "Neither do I."

"I'm glad to hear that," she murmured, her tongue flicking his chest. Helping her lover-husband off with his jeans, Mandy ventured, "Rule, there's something else. . . ."

When he was lying naked beside her, he urged, "What were you saying?" Without waiting for her to answer, he began to help her off with her clothes.

She luxuriated in the feeling of his hand sliding across her belly. His fingers dipped beneath the rim of her panties and after an erotic excursion that made Mandy's blood race, he gentled her panties off her legs.

She turned to him, her breathing erratic, and clung to his broad chest. "Darling, there's a children's hospital in Portland—the grounds and play yard are badly in need of flowers and shrubs, landscaping to brighten the children's stay. . . ."

Strong bands of iron that were Rule's arms, swept up from her rounded hips to hold her tightly to him. His deep chuckle rumbled through her whole body. "And you want to be the sunshine."

She nodded, her hair grazing his chin. "What do you think?"

He kissed her forehead. "I think one day you'll be Woman of the Year for your philanthropic work."

She craned her head back to see his face. "You've been so generous with your relatives—can we spare the money?"

He laughed outright. "We can."

Feeling giddy with happiness, she brazenly arched her hips to meet his tempting groin. He made a greedy sound in his throat. "Patience, my love."

"I need your undivided attention," she said, her hips teasing him into undisguised urgency.

"You'll have my undivided attention for a long time," he assured her, his voice husky.

"I'm counting on it." Her heart swelled with un-bounded happiness. "When did you say foaling season was?"

He cocked his head down, eyeing her strangely. "In early spring."

"It's your busy season?"

He nodded. "I hope so."

She reached up to caress his cheek, whispering, "It's going to be busier than you thought, darling. You see, next to the children's hospital is my doctor's office. I saw him today."

Rule stilled. "Are you all right?"

Her smile grew shy. "If you call being pregnant all right, then yes, I'm fine."

It took him a moment to grasp the import of her words. When he had, his face showed concern. He stroked her hair, his hand unsteady. "Are you happy about it?"

"Of course," she replied. "Aren't you?"

A tentative smile played at the corners of his mouth. "Mandy," he exhaled her name in a sigh, hugging her to him. "You couldn't have given me a better anniversary gift, believe me. I'm just not sure the world wants any more Danforth genes floating around."

Her laughter was light as she slid a hand down his side, across his hip until she was fondling her objective. "I don't know about the world—" she kissed his jaw "—but if it's left up to me, the Danforth species will be around for a long time."

"You're driving me crazy," he muttered urgently.

"Danforth curse—"

With a lusty moan, Rule slid up to blanket his wife, taking her with him to lofty heights that only those truly in love can explore. They were one in body and spirit, destined to spend their days and nights together here, on Barren Heath Isle, where they had found another heaven.

Janet DAILEY

THE MASTER FIDDLER

Jacqui didn't want to go back to college, and she didn't want to go home. Tombstone, Arizona, wasn't in her plans, either, until she found herself stuck there en route to L.A. after ramming her car into rancher Choya Barnett's Jeep. Things got worse when she lost her wallet and couldn't pay for the repairs. The mechanic wasn't interested when she practically propositioned him to get her car back—but Choya was. He took care of her bills and then waited for the debt to be paid with the only thing Jacqui had to offer—her virtue.

Watch for this bestselling Janet Dailey favorite, coming in June from Harlequin.

Also watch for *Something Extra* in August and *Sweet Promise* in October.

Harlequin Temptation dares to be different!

Once in a while, we Temptation editors spot a romance that's truly innovative. To make sure *you* don't miss any one of these outstanding selections, we'll mark them for you.

EDITOR'S
CHOICE

When the "Editors' Choice" fold-back appears on a Temptation cover, you'll know we've found that extra-special page-turner!

THE

Temptation

EDITORS

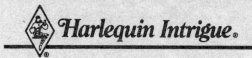

They went in through the terrace door. The house was dark, most of the servants were down at the circus, and only Nelbert's hired security guards were in sight. It was child's play for Blackheart to move past them, the work of two seconds to go through the solid lock on the terrace door. And then they were creeping through the darkened house, up the long curving stairs, Ferris fully as noiseless as the more experienced Blackheart.

They stopped on the second floor landing. "What if they have guns?" Ferris mouthed silently.

Blackheart shrugged. "Then duck."

"How reassuring," she responded. Footsteps directly above them signaled that the thieves were on the move, and so should they be.

For more romance, suspense and adventure, read Harlequin Intrigue. Two exciting titles each month, available wherever Harlequin Books are sold.